Erin turned on her back again and stared up at the two parallel bars of light dancing across the ceiling, reflections from the moonlight streaming through the open-draped window. Randi, in a hospital bed alone. Dying. No, that was not what the doctor had said. Not his phrase, dying. Could hold her in remission for years on drugs. In remission, she could live normally. Normal? Fifty percent had five-year survival rate. Maybe much longer. He'd even said they were starting to use the word "cure" now. Did she dare grasp hold of the hope he was holding out to them? Cured. Really cured? Five years. She'd be twenty. A year. No, she couldn't think of the shorter time. Why hadn't she stayed with her today during the tests? If she'd had any idea it was something like. . . .

SOMETHING FOR EVERYONE—
BEST SELLERS FROM ZEBRA!

WHAT PRICE LOVE by Alice Lent Covert (491, $2.25)
Unhappy and unfulfilled, Shane plunges into a passionate, all-consuming affair. And for the first time in her life she realizes that there's a dividing line between what a woman owes her husband and what she owes herself, and is willing to take the consequences no matter what the cost.

LOVE'S TENDER TEARS by Kate Ostrander (504, $1.95)
A beautiful woman caught between the bonds of innocence and womanhood, loyalty and love, passion and fame, is too proud to fight for the man she loves and risks her lifelong dream of happiness to save her pride.

WITHOUT SIN AMONG YOU (506, $2.50)
by Katherine Stapleton
Vivian Wright, the overnight success, the superstar writer who was turning the country upside down by exposing her most intimate adventures was on top of the world—until she was forced to make a devastating choice: her career or her fiance?

ALWAYS, MY LOVE by Dorothy Fletcher (517, $2.25)
Iris thought there was to be only one love in her lifetime—until she went to Paris with her widowed aunt and met Paul Chandon who quickly became their constant companion. But was Paul really attracted to her, or was he a fortune hunter after her aunt's money?

Available wherever paperbacks are sold, or order direct from the Publisher. Send cover price plus 40¢ per copy for mailing and handling to Zebra Books, 21 East 40th Street, New York, N.Y. 10016. DO NOT SEND CASH!

The Last Caress

Dianna Booher

ZEBRA BOOKS

KENSINGTON PUBLISHING CORP.

ZEBRA BOOKS

are published by

KENSINGTON PUBLISHING CORP.
21 East 40th Street
New York, N.Y. 10016

Copyright © 1980 by Dianna Booher

All rights reserved. No part of this book may be reproduced in any form or by any means without the prior written consent of the Publisher, excepting brief quotes used in reviews.

Printed in the United States of America

One

Erin negotiated her way down the icy sidewalk back to her office. Her first time to eat lunch out in over a month. She had eaten alone.

"Bring in that file on Kline, please," she said as she passed her secretary's desk. Freda tottered in with the file just as the phone buzzed. "Research . . . just a minute . . . your daughter." She handed the phone to Erin.

Erin covered the receiver. To Freda, "His application's not here. Would you get that too?" Back to the phone conversation. Randi was saying she was sorry to bother her at work. Erin grimaced; that sounded like something straight from her daddy's lips.

"It's okay. You're home early, aren't you?"

"Yeah. I didn't stay for practice. I'm not feeling too good again."

"I'm sorry, Hon. Can I bring you something on the way home? Some Bufferin?"

"No, we have some. . . . It's just that I don't

think I'm going to get to feeling good enough for Friday's game. Maybe the doctor could give me something to hurry me over whatever it is."

"Well, . . . sure. I'll call Dr. Bateman and see if he can work you in. Do you feel sick to your stomach?"

"Just a headache and my legs hurt. The same as yesterday."

"Okay, I'll call you back in a few minutes." Erin turned back to Freda. "A fifteen-year-old suggesting she go to the doctor's office?"

Three-fifteen was okay if she didn't mind waiting to be worked in. No way could she get through and be ready to go home then. She picked up the phone and started to dial Marsh.

But Randi had called *her*. She held the phone momentarily and then returned it to its cradle. Flipping through the Kline file again, she sighed. No, she'd promised him a definite answer today about the job. Two other projects—yesterday's unfinished work—lay on each side of the desk. Freda buzzed her to say Kline was on the phone again.

"Tell him I haven't made a decision yet, but . . . I'll be deciding this afternoon and I promise to phone him before I leave the office today." Polite, always polite. When she felt like telling him to forget it because he was pushing her. But he probably was the best qualified; he. . . . The doctor. She had to figure something out about the doctor's appointment and call Randi back.

Again she flipped through the work and

memos on her desk, pushed away and stood up. Two calls from New York for advance project reports were coming in this afternoon. She simply had to talk to the directors personally. She sauntered over to her bookcases, staring at the huge expanse of bound notebooks interspersed with knick knacks. Her daughter's picture came into focus. She picked it up and held it closer. Her hair had been cut since the photo was taken, but she still had the same half-turned up smile acquired when she first got her braces. Even though the orthodontist had since removed his handiwork, Randi clung to the new smile, a vital part of her new self-image. The frame was elaborate; Marsh and Randi had spent an entire day purchasing all the frames for both their offices and home. Marsh insisted that they find just the right one to pick up the highlights in her hair.

Erin's eyes fell to the backward-slanted scrawl across the bottom of the picture, "To Mom, Love Randi." Remembering the difference in the message written on the picture in her daddy's office—"To Dad with all my love, Randi"—reopened a wound she'd never mentioned, wouldn't ever mention. A subtle difference inscribed for all three to see, react to, accept. She had seen; she refused to accept.

Erin replaced the picture on the bookshelf and walked over to the window. Randi had called her first—just this once. What did other mothers do when they had to take children to the doctor or dentist? Take off or have their husbands to help out. She couldn't do either. Marsh was only too willing to come to the rescue. She should be grateful, shouldn't she? She stared out into the sunlight focusing on nothing until she became mesmerized by the brightness. Abruptly she turned back to her desk, picked up the phone and dialed.

"Chaplain's office, please."

Marsh came on the line. He was always in when she called, though he insisted he hated sitting in his office, that he'd rather be out with the patients and their families.

"Marsh, Randi called and said she was sick and needs to go to the doctor. I got her an appointment at three-fifteen, but it doesn't look like there's any way I can take her."

"I guess that's what she wanted. I just got back in the office and found a note saying she'd phoned."

Erin's expression drooped. Her husband continued, "So you want me to take her?"

"If you can get away. If not, I'll juggle something. It's just that I've been putting off making a decision about hiring someone and I need to get that vacancy filled today, and I have two long distance . . ."

"I'll take her."

"Are you sure? I could . . ."

"I said I'll take her."

Silence.

"I waited until 12:30 before ordering."

"Oh, . . . I didn't know we'd set up anything definite."

Pause.

"You'll have to pick up Randi at home. She left school early."

"Okay. I'll phone her and tell her to be ready when I . . ."

"I'll phone her. She's expecting me to call back."

"Whatever you say." He hung up.

Erin reopened the file on the desk and stared down into the gray haze, her eyes gliding from side to side while her mind failed to comprehend the words.

She'd done it again.

Erin arrived at the hospital before her husband and stopped in at Randi's room to say hello. Marsh's call earlier in the day that the doctor wanted to meet them at the clinic at six had upset her. The decision the day before to hospitalize Randi for tests had been a surprise too.

She'd offered to stay the night with her at the clinic. But Randi's response had been less than enthusiastic. "How much good would it do to go sit in my room while I'm ushered from lab to lab?" So, she'd reluctantly gone on to work. She'd phoned Randi from her office as soon as she was sure the hospital routine would have her awake. No answer in her room any time she'd called. The nurses' station kept saying she was here and there for this and that test. Erin was worried. Marsh's call after lunch hadn't helped matters.

"The doctor wants us to meet him at the clinic for a conference at 6:00," he'd spoken at his usual rapid-fire speed.

"Why? What's wrong that he can't give us the results over the phone?" she'd asked.

"I don't know, Erin. Just be there."

"I meant, is it something serious or the allergy thing again?"

"I told you all I know."

Silence.

"Do you want me to meet you at your office or at the clinic?"

"There."

Well, here she was—early. And early because she wanted to be. Randi sat propped up in bed watching an Andy Griffith rerun. She glanced toward the door as her mother walked in and then back to the TV.

"I've been calling all day. I kept getting the nurses," Erin said.

"One of 'em told me you called." Randi smiled and turned back to the program.

Erin glanced around the room. She noted the easily traceable brush strokes on the painted-over paneling. The drapes sprouted snags here and there on protruding pleats.

"Well, tell me, what all did they do to you?"

"A little bit of everything."

Erin waited for more details; there were none. Randi looked tired, listless. Erin wandered around the room, nervously fidgeting with the drapes, trying to pull them farther back. Five-thirty. She leaned back against the window casement and watched Randi watch TV.

The four gray filing cabinets came to mind again, as they had too frequently throughout the day. One decision, she'd almost blotted from her consciousness. At first, her resolution not to tell Marsh about the reports had wavered. But his resentment over the decision to stay in the Jackson area had held her back. She stood almost frozen now thinking of those gray cabinets as she had earlier in the day when she'd ushered Kline through the employee lounges, cafeteria, and various file rooms and departments. They had passed the dead file room. As she'd opened the door and gestured toward the cabinet-lined walls, her eyes had fallen on the four gray file cabinets on the left. She'd paused, holding the door ajar even though the new employee had wandered on down the hall back to his desk.

The file's contents held new significance in light of Randi's tests and Marsh's phone call at noon. But she was being silly to jump to conclusions. Obviously, the report was meaningless or the government would have done something, published something. If she had only told Marsh earlier, she could have completely dismissed it from her mind instead of repeatedly dredging it up. But what good would telling him have done? Why had she even bothered to go in there today? Kline wouldn't likely be retrieving things from that file room anyway.

Randi flipped the dial to another channel;

Erin refocused on the hospital surroundings.

"That's about all that's on this time of day, isn't it?" she asked Randi.

"What is?"

"Reruns."

"Yeah."

Randi became involved in the new program, buried her elbows back in the pillow. An amused half-smile spread across her face simultaneously with the canned laughter from the TV. Erin went back to her reverie. Five-fifty. It wasn't like Marsh to be late, not where Randi was involved. Maybe he'd gone by home first to change clothes. She traced his probable route by their Ponderine home. Once over the heated argument about settling down in the area, Marsh and she'd had no trouble agreeing on the house in Ponderine. It was as if the town had gradually evolved in the foothills just outside Jackson with no apparent forethought on the part of building contractors. Although Erin loved the wide open spaces and fresh air, she'd sold Marsh on the area by appealing to his need to think of himself as an outdoorsman.

He'd tried hard to project the "man's man" image ever since entering the chaplaincy. Though his opportunities for outings had declined as he got more settled into his career, he attempted to make at least a once-a-year campout. The macho image was the least he could do to pacify his parents who'd resented his studying theology and slighting his earlier inclination toward medicine.

Erin had neither participated in nor thwarted his efforts. She'd endured the first few roughing-it expeditions when Randi was younger but had withdrawn as soon as she could brush her own hair into dog-ears. Although Marsh and Randi had continued the mountain treks without her, they became fewer each year. Randi's interest in boys and basketball had triumphed. Marsh changed gears as Randi did year after year.

What did the doctor want to discuss? Marsh hadn't even been able to remember all the tests he had ordered. She wished she'd taken off yesterday and driven Randi to the doctor herself. If she'd had any idea it was going to be anything but the routine bout with allergy. . . . But the complaints were so vague. How could she have known it was something serious? Assuming the worst again. Marsh's constant assessment of her attitude.

A commercial. Randi flipped the channels again.

"You have a game Friday night?" Erin asked.

"Yes."

"Home or away?"

"Away. Hillsborough."

The program came back on; Erin dropped the conversation. She stood twirling the snags on the drapes, wadding the thread into tiny balls. The files again. Intimidating, accusing. No, she was not being rational. That was too long ago.

Marsh tapped against the half-opened door and pushed it open.

"How's my girl?" He came around the side of the bed to kiss his daughter on the cheek.

"I feel like Randi's bloodmobile."

"Oh, yeah?"

"I'm at least five pounds lighter."

"They took that much blood, uh? Well, with an extra few pounds off, that should make Michael sit up and take notice."

"Oh, Daddy," she brushed the remark aside.

"What else did they do to you?" Marsh repeated the earlier question, then glanced toward Erin and acknowledged her presence for the first time since entering the room.

"X-rays, blood tests, and two thousand other things I never heard of. Have you ever had to do all this?"

"I don't remember it if I did."

"Well, don't. It's not my idea of a party. Every time a nurse comes in here, she has a tray full of tubes."

There was a lull in the conversation. Erin walked nearer to where her husband stood.

"How was your day?" she asked.

"Okay. Yours?"

"Busy. Hired a new employee."

Marsh nodded and let an appropriate silence fall between them, then turned back to Randi.

"Is the doctor going to let you out of here by Friday's game?"

"I don't know why not. . . . You're going, aren't you?"

He nodded. "Is Michael going or are you going to ride back with me?"

"He's going. He'll follow the bus and then bring me on home."

Erin's eyes filled with tears. She turned on her heel and walked out into the hall. Marsh and Randi continued through the day's ordeal and the upcoming game plans.

The doctor was just coming down the hallway toward the consultation room. Erin stepped back into the room, summoned her husband, then headed for the conference room with Marsh behind her at least ten feet. She glanced back and slowed her pace, but he looked straight past her and kept his distance.

Two

The doctor stopped at the nurse's station before reaching the conference room and spoke to the Tillands momentarily.

"Go on in, right there to your left," he gestured with his pencil. "I've got to add a note to this chart; I'll be right with you."

Erin took a seat in the first chair. Marsh stood near the window, hands in his pants, jangling his keys. The jangling irritated Erin. Once when angry, she'd told him he'd been jangling keys since birth waiting for life to happen for him. He'd exploded; she'd apologized. She said nothing now. Waited.

"Doctors are all alike. You have to wait no matter what," Marsh said to himself as much as to Erin. Why couldn't he have told them what he had to say over the phone? Dramatics, always dramatic. They loved it. Keeping people waiting, afraid, until they laid out the plans for the miracle cure. Hero for the day. If he wanted to give her all those allergy tests, Randi surely would throw a fit.

Marsh turned away from the window and stared down at Erin. She sat slumped and worn-looking. Sensing his gaze on her, she looked up.

"Have you been over here all day?" she asked.

"On and off."

No further comment.

More or less his own boss, he made his own appointments, called on patients at his own pace. When he needed to be away, he merely left a number where he could be reached. Despite this freedom, Erin and he were rarely in touch during the day by phone or otherwise.

Marsh stood, still gazing down at his wife. She slipped her left high-heel off. For a brief moment, he felt the urge to reach down and massage her foot.

The foot-massage ritual had been initiated after Erin's first day on the job with Bending and Dowden. She'd immediately formulated plans to start back to college at night to finish her degree so she could "go right to the top," as she'd phrased it. Other people collect stamps; Erin played with statistics. She quoted the figures to him—how many women executives there were in top management positions and how much education and experience were required to get there.

The foot massaging was still a ritual, but not so frequent as it had been. He'd needed to do it for her in the beginning to have a part in her success. Now she needed it. The sentiment, if not the massage.

The doctor came in and spoke to both the Tillands, whom he knew only on a professional basis. Young and good-looking, he wore a discreet mustache. He had always had Randi's confidence. Marsh took a seat beside his wife on the couch and waited for the doctor to begin.

"Erin, Marsh, I'm afraid to say that I've got some very bad news. These tests today have confirmed beyond a shadow of a doubt what I suspected yesterday when you brought Randi in. . . . She's a very sick girl. . . . She has leukemia."

Randi was leaning on the counter at the nurse's station looking pretty well recuperated from the day's ordeal, when a tall, curly-headed young man stepped off the elevator later that night. She bounded toward him before he reached the nurse's station.

"Hey, what's the rush?" Mike tried to put his arm around her, but she steered him into her room.

"It's after visiting hours, that's what. The sergeant down there definitely isn't the understanding type." She closed the door and hopped back into the middle of the bed pulling the sheet over her feet.

"You don't look too sick to me."

"I'm not. But those tests about made me that way. What're you doing stopping by here so late? It's ten o'clock."

"I know. I couldn't get everything done at the library."

"What're you doing at the library?"

"Ladimer told us we had to have about four hundred sources for that paper. But I got tired copying all the call numbers. Anyway, when you getting out?"

"The next day or two, I think. Mother and Daddy weren't sure when they came by. They said I'd have to stay long enough to get started on some medicine."

"What you got?"

"Anemia. Daddy said that's why they took so much blood."

"Is that serious?"

"No. Kinda like tired blood. But you know my folks. They already looked worried to death when they came by. Every time I sneeze, they treat me like I had pneumonia."

"I told you being an only child wasn't all it was cracked up to be."

Randi looked down at her hands and forearms. "I knew it had to be something like that. You wouldn't believe the needle holes I got." She yanked up her robe sleeves and exposed the beige plastic dots scattered on the insides of both arms.

Mike bent over and kissed her.

"Feel better?"

"Improving rapidly, thank you."

He kissed her again.

"What do they do for it? Besides drain all your blood?"

19

"Give me medicine. They said the doctor was going to start me on an antibiotic tonight. As soon as they get the right dosage figured out, I can go home. Daddy said I *might* have to stay around a few days longer to make sure I don't get sick from the medicine. But the only time I get sick is riding in your truck."

Mike smirked and shifted his weight from one foot to the other.

Randi rattled on, "But the clincher is that I have to come back to the lab once a week for them to take a blood count to see how I'm doing."

"Can you play Friday night?"

"I don't know. Would you believe I forgot to ask?"

"No."

"Well, I did. I'll find out in the morning.

"Your parents going?"

"Daddy."

"Well, I knew he'd go. I meant both of them. Is it okay if I bring you home?"

"Yeah. He'll fix it with Mother. She was in here when I mentioned it this afternoon. She didn't say anything."

"Come on sixteenth birthday."

"It doesn't hurt you to have to wait for an answer. Makes me a prized possession." She smacked a kiss into the air. "Just think what kind of wife I'll make some day. I've been raised right by the book."

Mike grinned.

"Anyway, the way I feel right now, I'm not

up to another twenty-eight pointer. Holden's gonna be harder to beat. You remember that center, don't you?"

"Well, I wasn't particularly watching her if that's what you mean." Mike swung his western hat round and round on his thumb.

The door swung open; "sergeant" plowed through with a medicine tray.

"I didn't know we had visitors." She held a tray precariously at the edge of Randi's bed and turned to Mike. "Visiting hours are over." She gave the words a slight punch as they rolled out over her colorless lips.

"I just got here."

The nurse pushed the pills and water toward Randi never bothering to answer. Leaving, she paused at the door and held it open. Mike squashed the paper cup he'd been holding and tossed it in the wastebasket.

"Call you tomorrow." He brushed by the ample figure standing in the doorway.

At midnight Erin turned out the light and pulled the blanket up over her with little hope of sleep. Marsh lay with hands behind his head, staring up at the ceiling. Both silent now after hours of talk and tears. Erin listened to the slow steady rhythm of her husband's breathing.

"Are you sure we did the right thing?" Erin broke the silence.

"What?"

"Not telling Randi?"

"Yes."

"I'm not."

Silence.

"Dr. Batemen said she'd have to know sooner or later," Erin said.

"Later. When she's in remission. Then she can . . . take it."

Erin fluffed up the pillow and turned to face her husband; he still stared straight ahead into the shadows. She studied his profile; his expression was frozen, his eyes refusing to blink.

"What was the name of that drug?" he asked after a minute.

"I can't remember. Everything he said seems like a blur."

"They do that on purpose."

"Do what?"

"Talk in circles. So they can play God with the miracles."

Silence.

"I wonder how sick it'll make her?"

"He said 'pretty nauseated.'"

"But just until her system's used to it," Marsh added.

"Yeah."

Erin turned on her back again and stared up at the two parallel bars of light dancing across the ceiling, reflections from the moonlight streaming through the open-draped window. Randi, in a hospital bed alone. Dying. No, that was not what the doctor had said. Not his phrase, dying. Could hold her in remission for years on drugs. In remission, she could live normally. Normal? Fifty percent had five-year survival rate. Maybe much longer. He'd even said they were starting to use the word "cure" now. Did she dare grasp hold of the hope he was holding out to them? Cured. Really cured? Five years. She'd be twenty. A year. No, she couldn't think of the shorter time. Why hadn't she stayed with her today during the tests? If she'd had any idea it was something like. . . .

"She'll be home in a few days. Maybe Tuesday or Wednesday," Marsh said aloud.

"Maybe, . . . but if this drug doesn't work. . . ."

"We'll try another one. It's just a matter of time."

The silence was profound. Erin knew what he'd meant—a matter of time until they found the right drug for her. She could sense Marsh's own recoil as he realized what he'd said. Would the rest of their lives be tiptoeing over and around such words, thoughts, future plans?

Erin glanced at the clock as she turned over for what seemed like the hundredth time. Two-thirty.

"Are you asleep?"

"No."

The light from the digital alarm clock further illuminated the already dimly-lit room. Moonlight. For such a reason she'd convinced Marsh to stay out here in this part of the country. To be away from city smog, noise, traffic, she'd said. To enjoy the outdoors without having to drive miles to get to fresh air. With those reasons, he'd had no complaint. But despite her explanations, Marsh and she had both known the primary, decisive reasons—her job and school. She'd followed him around the country the first two years of their marriage while he finished college, did his graduate work, and investigated various hospital situations and counseling centers. It'd been she who'd insisted it would be foolish to leave a job which held such good possibilities for her. And finishing her degree would add considerably to her chances for advancement. She knew Marsh had resented having to consider such things. He'd held her small daughter up to her, then, as the sole reason she shouldn't take her work seriously.

But Erin sensed that the resentment on his part involved more than the working-mom syndrome. And that unacknowledged sentiment smouldered on the back burner, ready to be moved to the front at the least irritation or conflict of schedules.

The two parallel beams of moonlight slid off the ceiling as a passing car blotted them out.

"But remission isn't 'cured' exactly, is it?" Marsh asked.

"He said it was when there was absolutely no sign of the disease."

"What's the difference?"

"In what?"

"Between remission and cured?"

"How long the remission lasts, I guess."

Another long silence. Four o'clock. Erin

stared at the faint ouline of the tall, narrow bachelor bureau occupying the adjacent wall. Files. It'd been so long ago since she'd read those reports. Maybe she didn't remember accurately. No, she remembered. She was the reason . . . she was the one . . . she had done this to Randi as surely as if. . . . She clenched her teeth so hard that sharp piercing pains penetrated her jaws. Tears again slid out of the corners of her eyes and rolled back into her hair.

Marsh reached over and pulled her closer to him. His breath felt warm against her neck; his arm across her, heavy. How could he know? What if he really knew what she'd done. Or hadn't done. Never, never had she really believed that her own daughter. . . . How could she have known?

"Isn't that what Graham's son had?"

"Yes."

Three

The next morning Erin woke to find Marsh gone. She felt as if she were waking from heavy sedation, yet surprised that she'd fallen asleep at all. She dragged herself out of bed and pulled up the blanket and spread. Marsh must have been called out early again, but surely she couldn't have slept through the phone call.

She dialed Randi.

"Did I wake you up?"

"Kind of."

"I'm sorry. I just wanted to know how you were feeling."

"Okay. Except they make too much noise around here. They came in at six and woke me up to take my temperature. I just now went back to sleep."

"That's a hospital for you." Keep the tone light. "Well, go back to sleep. I'll phone you later."

Erin dressed and left for work without

breakfast. Slowly, ever so slowly, she navigated the slightly icy highway. The habitually bad roads had never bothered her until now. Today her attention had to be captured and forced to line out a path into the city.

"Morning. You're sure up and around early this morning," Freda greeted Erin as she brushed past her at the coffeemaker.

Good morning. Her child was dying. Was it morning? Erin smiled tightly and glanced at her watch. Seven-forty. No machines clinking. No chatter. The office presented a vaguely ominous atmosphere which Erin had forgotten since her early morning hours as secretary with Bending and Dowden. Only a few hearty souls—those who had to carpool with a spouse or friend— were on the premises.

"Hi. How are you?" Mack spoke.

"Fine." Erin smiled again. They were just standing there—Mack, Freda, June. Talking. As if the world could go on as usual. Her daughter had leukemia, and they talked about the icy streets.

Erin deposited her coat and purse in the closet and stood behind her desk motionless, paralyzed by indecision. Now was as good a time as any. She took the keys from the middle drawer and hurried down the hall toward the back office, unlocked and re-locked the door as she entered. The room smelled musty. It was off-limits for the custodians. A layer of dust covered the top of each cabinet and the handles. The heavy file drawers squeaked as she pulled them out one by one. The first cabinet proved empty. She moved to the second and repeated the search. It had to be in one of the first four; she distinctly remembered the gray cabinets as opposed to the army green ones, which lined the other three walls.

Why was she being so secretive, she questioned herself. Who was going to accuse her? They didn't even know Randi was . . . sick. Probably no one else in the office even knew about the research project. For ten years those files had been collecting dust, only disturbed occasionally when someone from across the street needed an old file and sent a messenger over to retrieve a boxload. Duplicates of almost every research finding filed here probably lay in various offices across the country. Bending certainly couldn't guarantee security on everything they did. Nor was there reason to do so on ninety percent of their work. Only rarely did companies sub-contract jobs to them—to use their systems and manpower—when security was part of the arrangement.

Such had been the case with the research report she now wanted. It would be filed under the government subcontracts somewhere. Her search continued through drawer after drawer.

She reappeared in the hallway, clutching two folders to her breast. Her face was drawn as she hurried back to her side of the building.

Safely inside her office, she locked the door, something she couldn't remember doing since she moved into the position three years ago.

People were at work now. Machines going, telephones ringing, stenographers laughing. She couldn't be disturbed, or anyone seeing her face would sense her anguish. Marsh had always told her if she ever wanted to keep a secret, she'd have to close her eyes as well as her lips. If only it could have been a secret from her. Guilt hung heavily about her, as if a heavy cape were about her shoulders, dragging her down.

She opened the first folder and flipped through, finding all the preliminary reports on the researchers involved and the procedures. The second folder contained the finished, typed draft ready for publication.

Erin read the report.

> Additional information has accumulated on the effects of exposure to ionizing radiation on the human organism. The present report deals with the early and delayed hematologic effects of longterm exposure to low dose rates. The major sources of this long-term exposure are nuclear testing explosions near residential sites in Perry, Unity, and Vale counties.

She skimmed the details and terms of the data-collecting procedures. Her eyes fell frozen over the concluding paragraphs of the report:

> As previously proven, external radiation in large amounts, delivered at low dose rates to the entire body or to a large segment of

the bone marrow is leukemogenic in man. Young children and teenagers comprise the most susceptible segment of the population to long-term exposure. Present evidence is insufficient to prove or disprove the hypothesis of a "threshhold" for radiation in man. Data collected in this investigation, however, reveals marked increase in thyroid and leukemogenic cancer in persons in Perry, Unity, and Vale counties. Persons, especially young children and teens, residing in these above mentioned counties are six times as likely as the general population to develop leukemia and thyroid cancer.

Therefore, we recommend that the radiation-leukemia and radiation-thyroid cancer relationship be further investigated, and in each case legislators and the general public must weigh the benefits associated with radiation against the health hazards for area residents.

Erin stared blankly at the page for a long time. She had stayed. Randi had leukemia because she had stayed. The words on the page coalesced into a gray haze before her eyes.

She had not forgotten the first time she'd read the report. She'd been clearing out her supervisor's "out" basket, looking for a missing letter. Not finding it there, she'd begun a quick search through the papers stacked here and there on his desk. "Leukemia-Radiation Study" the title page read. She'd picked it up and leafed through it casually until coming to the concluding paragraphs. This was . . . was unbelievable! Here. Right where she had insisted that Marsh and she stay while she finished night school.

She'd laid the report back on the desk but was not about to forget its contents. Wonder what they were going to do about it? People were really going to be angry when they found out!

When Isaac Morton, her supervisor, had come in later in the morning, she'd followed him into his office.

"Mr. Morton, I was looking for that Crane letter I left on your desk for your signature. . . ."

"I signed it. I'm sure." He started to shuffle papers from side to side.

"Yes. I found it."

He stopped and looked up, waiting for her to finish.

"Uh. . . . When I was looking around for it, I came across that leukemia report." She pointed toward the folder.

Her boss stood still behind his desk studying her face calmly as if waiting for her to get to the point.

"I didn't know about it—the study project. I just can't believe it."

"Yes. . . . Quite an interesting study."

"When . . . was it done? Did we do it?"

"Shut the door behind you, will you?" Morton eased his large frame down in the chair behind him. "Yes, we helped with it. Finished it a couple days ago."

"What's going to happen when people hear about it? I can just imagine! I mean, what do you do if you've got a business here?"

"Erin, these reports aren't conclusive." His tone became patronizing. "Not as conclusive as they sound."

"What do you mean?"

"Well, . . . other firms have done similar studies. Some of their findings negate, or at least make doubtful, the same conclusions this report shows." He paused and lit his cigar, then continued. "Who knows what the real facts are? Who knows?"

"But that says that people are six times as likely to get cancer. That's scary! Surely they're going to keep studying it and come to some conclusions. I mean. . . ."

"I'm sure they will. I'm sure they will. But it'll take years. Years." He sang the word.

"What are they going to do in the meantime?"

"Nothing. Not yet."

"But at least it looks like they'll tell people what they found out so far?"

"Now, Erin, you can't tell people something like that. Why, they'd go crazy. Be scared stiff."

"I know. . . ."

"People can't be reasonable. This report isn't conclusive. It's somebody's theory with a few isolated facts to back it up."

"But I thought we were in on the research. I

thought we did it right? Reputably?"

"Of course, we did. I'm just saying that this report isn't enough evidence to be meaningful in light of other studies done years ago." Mr. Morton's voice sounded harsher as if he were tired of making the same point to this naive young woman.

"Sit down, Erin. Sit down."

She took a seat on the sofa near the window and waited for further explanation to what seemed incomprehensible.

"Look, even if this report was published—we went to the press with it—what would people do?"

"Move."

"No, they wouldn't." He took a longer draw on his cigar. "They'd stay right where they are. Their lives are here. Businesses. Family. People don't pick up and move on a whim."

"But this is cancer!"

"Sure it is. But it wouldn't be any different. They've been telling Californians for years that they're sitting on a powder keg, that an earthquake is going to split 'em off right out into the ocean. How many people are leaving California?" He paused. Then, "And what about people who live in flood areas. They get flooded every two or three years. What do they do? Rebuild. Stay right there. . . . People are funny, really strange." He took another long draw on his cigar and studied Erin's face.

"I guess so," she shrugged, "but I still think if they knew about this, they'd . . . they'd . . .

do something."

"And you're forgetting the most important thing. It's not our decision. We're not the ones to say when and if this is released. That's Uncle Sam's affair."

Erin nodded again. Although not in on the project, she was aware that two government men had spent the better part of two months in and out of their offices. But as a secretary, she hovered only on the periphery of big projects.

"But don't you have any authority on things like that? What would keep you from calling the newspapers anyway?"

"My job." His eyes took on a strange gleam as he tapped his cigar against the ashtray. "You don't think I could expect to keep my job if I turned over every report that came through my hands? That's not my responsibility. My decision. Most especially when the government's involved. You learn that, Erin. You learn that really quick." He leaned back in his chair, hands behind his head.

Erin said nothing.

"You're finishing school. You're ready to move up."

"I hope so."

"You are. You will. But let me tell you right now, in this department, you can't—you aren't free to use the information we come up with for your own use. It's like stealing a typewriter. They hire you to gather the data, Erin. Gather the data. They make the decisions. If you plan to go anywhere, you'd better remember that."

Erin had left his office in a perplexed state. Sitting at her typewriter the rest of the day, she had typed mechanically, her thoughts miles away. Her own daughter. If there was anything to the reports, it was too late now. Randi was five; she'd already had years to be exposed to the radiation.

But Mr. Morton had insisted the reports were inconclusive. Maybe she would read the whole report again herself tomorrow or the next day when she got a chance. That chance never came.

The two government men had come back later that week, Morton had told her offhandedly, to get all the copies of the report, presumably to correlate with other aspects of the research project handled by other firms. Then, Morton had intimated, they would be publishing some sort of statement or article about the findings.

No article or newspaper story ever appeared. Six months passed. Still no article.

Erin had almost revealed the findings to Marsh so many times. Yet, something always held her back. She knew he'd throw it up to her. Blame her for wanting to stay in the area. How could she tell him this? What good would it do now?

Day after day, month after month dragged on in silence. With each month's passing, the situation seemed less ominous. The government's silence on the matter seemed to indicate that her supervisor was right—that the reports were meaningless, inconclusive.

It was not until three years later that she'd learned a copy of the report was still in their files. She had never understood how her old supervisor—then promoted to a completely new division—got away with keeping the copy. But there it was. Filed away in the inactive files room. Morton had often boasted that nobody told him what he could or couldn't keep a copy of. Finding that copy in the file drawer had made a believer of her. She even forgot the report for months at a time. Until some joke, some newsreel, some magazine article brought it to mind.

Ten years now. And she hadn't done a thing about it. Her own daughter one of the statistics. It was too late to do anything. Say anything. A flood of grief from yesterday afternoon rolled over her.

Erin closed the file folder mechanically, stacking each page perfectly in line with the preceding page and turned to the scene outside her office window. The sunlight reflecting on the remaining inch of snow which blanketed the manicured lawns of surrounding buildings streamed in. Two birds chirped on the highline wire descending from the corner of the tallest building to Bending and Dowden. Traffic was minimal. A petite brunette climbed out of her parked car and lifted a small child from his infant seat. The mother eased the child to the freshly shoveled sidewalk and permitted him to dash off after the bird a few feet beyond him. Both arms in the air, the delighted toddler lunged forward in pursuit of his prey. The mother stood watching her squealing child as he breathed the air of this crisp January day.

Four

Marsh pulled on his shoes and tied the laces hurriedly. "Come on. I'll be outside in the car."

"I'll be out in a minute." Randi continued to rummage through her drawer for socks. She plopped down on the side of her bed to put on her tennis shoes. She'd come home from the hospital three days after starting on the medication for her "anemia," but she'd been nauseated, a predicted side-effect of the antibiotic, for the week she'd been home.

Erin, still in her robe, passed by her daughter's room, surprised to see her up so early.

"Well, you look like you're feeling pretty good this morning."

"Yeah. I am." Randi straightened the bedspread again and scurried around the corner to the hall bathroom to brush her teeth.

"What are you brushing your teeth now for? Have you already had breakfast?"

"A bowl of cereal."

"Where's your dad? He up, too?" Erin turned around toward the den but couldn't see her husband.

"Yeah. We both ate." Randi slung the water out of her toothbrush and replaced it on the wall rack.

Erin followed her back to the doorway of her room and stood watching as she pulled on a long-sleeved shirt over the sleeveless one she already wore. The sleeves hung a little too short. Still growing. But Erin knew better than to mention her height; ever since Randi had passed 5'5", she'd been self-conscious about it. Erin had never let her own 5'8" bother her. A model's figure her parents had always called it. Despite Erin's example, Randi considered her height a detriment to all causes but basketball. Erin studied her daughter's face. She definitely looked better; the dark circles under her eyes, gone.

"Well, what are you planning for the day now that you feel like a million?"

"Daddy and I are going down to the gym to work out."

Erin stared at her daughter. "What?"

"Daddy got the key from the janitor, and Coach said it was all right if I worked out this morning. He even left a couple balls out for us."

"Honey, . . ." Erin hated the fear that was creeping over her. And rage, at Marsh for telling her she could go through with it. She began again.

"I don't think it's such a good idea to get that much exercise so soon after you've . . . started on that medicine."

"I feel fine."

"I know you do now. . . . But a workout may set you back where you were a few days ago. I think . . ."

"Mother, please."

"In a couple of weeks, you'll feel more like . . ."

"Dr. Bateman said I could do anything I felt like, remember?"

"Sure. But he didn't mean a basketball workout."

"How do you know?" Randi snapped.

"Hey, come on," Marsh yelled through the back door. "The car's warm. What are you doing in here?"

Neither Erin or Randi answered him; both stood glaring at the other.

Marsh closed the door and came through the kitchen into the den, his jacket and cap covered with tiny wet spots.

"Is it snowing?"

"Just beginning. A few flakes now and then." Then turning to Randi, "Come on, the car's warm."

"I was just telling her that I don't think she's quite up to a workout yet. And besides that, the weather's bad. The doctor told her to be careful about catching a cold."

Erin's eyes pleaded with her husband to agree, to support her in this. So many times he'd been a mother-hen about their daughter's health. Now that such precaution was called for, he seemed oblivious to the matter.

"She says she feels fine. I wouldn't take her if she didn't."

"Erin's face reddened. "She may feel fine, but . . ." She felt awkward trying to discuss the issue in Randi's presence. She'd tried to conceal her anxiety in the last two weeks so as not to give Randi cause for suspicion. But how could she persuade her of the need to be cautious yet keep the truth from her? Why wasn't Marsh acting like a father rather than a school kid calling his friend out to play?

"The doctor told her she could do whatever she felt like," Marsh still insisted.

"Yeah. And I'm already out of shape just lying around after school. I can't just walk out on the court next Tuesday night and play like always." Randi's tone softened to a plea. "I'll take it easy. . . . Daddy may not be off tomorrow."

Erin stood motionless, her eyes stricken, torn between saying what Randi wanted to hear and what she felt was necessary due to the doctor's warnings about her catching cold. An idea flashed.

"Why don't you call the doctor and ask him about it?"

"Oh, Motherrr." Randi chucked her jacket

on the back of the chair and sat down. "He won't even be in on Saturday."

"Yes, he will. His office is open until 1:00."

"If it'll make your mother feel better, go ahead and call," Marsh said.

Randi went to the phone. "He's gonna think I'm a real pest."

"Hurry up and call," Marsh said again. "We've already wasted half an hour."

Erin's eyes devoured him. He actually was encouraging her in this, wasn't he? Acting like nothing was wrong—like if they didn't talk about it, it would all go away. Well, he wasn't going to do this to her. She'd always been the one to have to make Randi eat her spinach while he took her to the circus.

Marsh poured himself another cup of coffee and sat sipping it while Randi made the call.

Fear of what might happen if Randi worked out and anger at Marsh for encouraging her fought for control over Erin's mind. She could tell from Randi's end of the conversation things weren't going as planned. But if the doctor would give his permission?

"Whoppeee," Randi shouted, snapped her fingers, and clapped her palms. "He said go ahead. Do anything I wanted, just don't overdo it and get too tired."

"Feel better?" Marsh asked Erin as he ushered Randi out the door, not waiting for an answer.

Erin stood frozen in the same spot until they were out the door. Then she moved to the kitchen window and watched them brushing snow off as they took refuge in the warm car. She saw Marsh throw his tennis racket over into the backseat. He'd been promising to teach her to play for years. She'd finally quit asking. Randi's eager grin became visible through the windshield. Fifteen years old and still as excited about a morning's basketball workout as a date. In another year or two. . . , the thought stopped in midstream.

In the two weeks since the diagnosis, Marsh had refused to discuss the issue with her. His way of "handling" things—just don't admit they're real.

Erin permitted him his silence about Randi for reasons of her own. The report still consumed her thoughts. One day she would decide definitely to call someone, some official to tell them about the file and the facts. Then the day would somehow drag to an end, and she'd hide behind the promise of tomorrow to make the revelation that she feared would irreparably separate her from her husband and daughter.

The rest of her waking hours she agonized over Randi's welfare. Nevertheless, she clasped on to the dream, surrounded by fear, which was shared by so many other parents of such children—that their child would somehow be different, that she'd stay in remission for years, that a new drug would be discovered which would put an end to all their fears. Was it a dream or a real hope? Erin didn't allow herself many fantasies, but this one she clung to.

The doctor had advised them to let her go. To let her live the best life she knew how. Erin's habitual insistence on facing reality gave way that morning, as she watched her husband and daughter drive off to the gym, to a determination that Randi's illness would be different—that life would still proceed as planned.

There would be only one new twist. She would not let Marsh shut her out any longer. She would work her way into Randi's life. No matter what it took.

Erin washed her hair, straightened the house, and played the piano until Randi and her dad came in. She met them at the door.

"How did it go?"

"Great," Randi answered. "But I'm out of shape already."

"Not much, she isn't. Don't let her kid you. She'll be back to normal by Tuesday's game," her dad disputed her.

"Did you just shoot baskets, or what?"

"Started out that way. I practiced free throws until Daddy got too lazy to rebound. Then we practiced my hook shot. My left's still too sloppy to be much of a threat."

Randi plunged on into the room between Marsh and Erin and flopped in a kitchen chair. Erin backed up to the bar, stood first on one foot, then the other. A free day, not to be wasted. She waited; no one spoke, offered an agenda.

Then, "What do you have planned now . . . for the rest of the day?" Erin asked.

"Well, we thought about tennis. . . ." Erin's face stiffened. "But Daddy said he was too tired, and it was too cold. We're going into Jackson and walk around the mall a while."

"Oh."

Silence.

"I don't have anything particular planned. . . ." Keep the tone casual, no big deal. "I might go along, too."

"Okay," Randi said. "We thought you'd probably have to go in to the office a while."

Erin searched their faces for other meaning but found nothing there. "I'll fix us an early lunch. How about a ham sandwich?"

"We were gonna get pizza on the way," Randi said.

"Oh, . . . all right. . . . Well, then. . . I guess I'm ready whenever you two are."

"I'm gonna take a quick shower first." Randi darted off toward the bathroom.

"I've got to have one, too. So don't use all the hot water." Marsh swatted at the air behind her.

Erin backed up and sat down on the piano bench facing her husband, who'd leaned back in his lounge chair and picked up the morning paper. Marsh read intently; Erin sat watching him. His blonde hair still looked thick despite the crushed effect from the tobogganing cap. She started to ease over into his lap. Then remembering their earlier discussion, she tossed the thought aside. She could hear Randi's shower running.

"How did she feel this morning?"

"What?" Marsh looked up.

"I said, 'How did Randi feel this morning?'"

"She told you, didn't she?"

Erin clenched her teeth, felt her jaws tighten. "I thought maybe you could tell otherwise."

"No, I couldn't. A little slow getting started, but after that she was her old self again."

"Her old self?"

"Yes. What did you expect? The doctor wouldn't have let her go if it wasn't okay."

"Yes, but . . ." She lapsed back against the keyboard. He went back to the paper. She studied the features of his face one by one. Nose, average. Jaw, angular. Eyebrows, light brown, bushy, slightly arched over the pupil. Crow's feet around the eyes. His square forehead, bordered evenly. No furrow. A complete mask. Always.

"Why are you acting so . . . so . . ." she groped for the right word.

"So what?"

"So . . . I don't know. . . . As if nothing's wrong?"

"What do you want me to do? Sit around and think about what she can't do, what might happen if . . . if she has a nosebleed, or takes pneumonia, or a dozen other things the doctor said to watch out for. Is that what you want me to do? Sit around and think about it?"

"No, but you're acting like . . . like if you don't think about it, it'll go away. . . ."

"I am not."

"Yes, you are, Marsh. You *are*. You have to face the fact that . . ."

"Erin, I can and I am facing facts. I really don't need this lecture, if you don't mind."

He looked back to the paper for a moment, then up again. "Look, I'm sorry. I know you're worried. And I'm sorry I didn't mention the workout to you earlier. I didn't think you'd be home this morning or I'd have said something."

Erin nodded, accepted his apology.

"But we can't just keep her under lock and key."

"That's not what I want either. I just think . . ."

The shower stopped running. Marsh snapped his head in the direction of the bathroom as if to command his wife to drop the subject.

Erin turned back to the keyboard and pressed the keys loudly, then eased her tone to the usual barely-audible level. She heard him fold the paper and leave the room. A few minutes later his shower was running. She stopped playing and sat poised on the edge of the bench, hands resting lightly over the keys.

Randi came back into the room, took a seat on the couch, and flipped on the television. Startled, Erin slid around on the piano bench to face the television screen along with her daughter. Randi looked tired, very tired. The early morning eagerness, gone. But Erin suppressed the urge to suggest that she lie back and rest a few minutes before the shopping trip.

"Is Mike coming over tonight?" she asked instead.

"Huh?" Randi never took her eyes off the screen. A performer swung around and around the parallel bars and dropped to the floor in perfect position. Applause rose from the crowd.

Erin asked again, "Is Mike coming by tonight?"

"Yes."

"You hadn't mentioned it. I didn't know."

"Thought I had."

"Maybe you did and I forgot," Erin lied.

"Is it okay?"

"Sure. If your dad doesn't have anything else planned."

Both sat in silence. Randi watched the score cards as the judges held up their tabulations; Erin watched Randi. What would she say if she knew about the research? If she knew her own mother . . .

"Okay." Marsh wandered into the room. He had on a navy velour shirt, matching plaid pants. The "woodsy" scent of his cologne filled the room. "I'm ready. Let's hit the road."

Randi switched off the TV, grabbed her jacket, and was out the door before either parent.

"Should I lay something out to thaw for

dinner?" Erin asked Marsh on the way out.

"Always thinking ahead, aren't you? That's a working Mom for you."

Erin didn't respond.

"I don't care. I guess we'll plan to be back here for dinner. Randi's got a date at 7:00. Michael's taking her to Flanagin's to eat."

Erin turned back to the freezer and laid a package of hamburger in the sink.

Five

Erin made it a point to plan her work so she'd be available to attend Randi's game, her first since the diagnosis and quickly achieved remission. The opposing team had forfeited Tuesday's game due to the heavy accumulation of snow over the weekend. Randi had resumed her usual hectic pace at school. Her weekly trips to the out-patient clinic proved the only visible signs of her struggle with illness. No signs of suspicion.

"Are you going to the game tonight?" Marsh asked Erin at breakfast.

"Yes, I think so. . . . It's here, isn't it?"

"No. We go to Dawson."

Erin thoughtfully tore her toast in half, took another bite.

"Are you still going?"

"Yes."

She resented his manner, his feigned surprise.

She'd missed only four games of the season. She stacked the dishes into the dishwasher and left for work. Throughout the day the fear of what might happen if Randi were injured kept nagging for attention. The doctor had warned that leukemia patients bleed freely at times and that losing too much blood before they could get to the hospital might prove fatal. Erin shut the thought away; Randi was in remission now.

Marsh drove Randi to the school to catch the team bus and returned home for Erin. "I'm back. Let's go," he shouted in the back door.

Erin added another touch of perfume and joined her husband in the car. "Do you think any of the other parents might want to ride with us?" she added.

"Oh, I don't know. Most of them follow the bus. I can't stand that."

"Why not?"

"Reminds me of a bunch of sheep"

Silence.

"We should have called someone else to go," Erin said.

"Who?"

"I don't know. The Gabriels, maybe. Stan and I need to talk about the Hile project anyway."

"I couldn't take a whole evening with Margie."

"Well, who then?"

"Who what?"

"Who could we ask?"

"It's too late to . . ."

"I don't mean to go to the game. I mean sometime. Who could we get together with—go out to dinner?"

Marsh shrugged.

"Isn't there somebody at the hospital?"

"Not really."

"We haven't been out to dinner with anybody in ages. We go from one extreme to the other."

Silence.

"Mark and Mary Ann Templar?" Erin asked.

"No. I don't think so."

"How about Steve and Sandy? Isn't that their names?"

"They're having marital problems. He was in to see me a few days ago. Wants to start counseling."

"And?"

"And you know I don't want to mix the relationship up—being out together socially."

Erin dropped the matter and settled back into the seat. Maybe she'd get together with Gloria for lunch next week. She hadn't talked to her in over a month.

They'd met through a mutual acquaintance at work when Erin had asked around about a piano teacher for Randi. Gloria was in her late twenties and single; Randi and she'd hit it off from the very beginning. And visiting casually before and after the lessons, Erin and she had become friends. Erin missed the weekly chats, which sometimes had stretched to the length of the piano lesson itself. On such occasions, Randi, sitting in the car doing her homework, let her know about it. Since the lessons had stopped, they saw each other infrequently. Lunch now and then.

Erin gazed out into the velvety darkness. The lessons seemed eons ago. She'd been the one to complain when Randi had wanted to quit; Marsh had agreed with Randi that she "just didn't have time for music now that she was in junior high." Randi had quit. It wouldn't be a long trip—twenty-two miles. She turned back to Marsh.

"How was your day?" she asked.

"Okay. Yours?"

"The usual." Then "Kenneth Kline, the guy I hired a couple weeks back, is working out okay. I had my doubts, but he knows his way around already. I put him on an assignment I'd hoped for him to finish in a week, and he handed me the results in two days."

"Good."

Silence.

Erin turned her attention straight ahead. An approaching car light lit up their front seat. Then darkness again. She could never tell whether he was interested in her work anymore. At first he'd pried every detail from her, enjoying every decision she'd struggled with. He'd helped her sort out the alternatives and come up with a viable solution, then anxiously waited for her report about how the situation developed. Now, he seldom questioned her about what Bending and Dowden was up to and rarely responded to her offering such minutia.

"How's the older lady at the hospital . . . the Catholic lady, Mrs. . . ."

"Mrs. Wibble?"

"Yes."

"About the same."

"Does she have any family?"

"One son. Out of state. He's been here a couple of times."

"I guess it must be hard to . . . ," she had to finish, "die alone." The words sent a shudder through Erin and did much worse to Marsh. He kept his eyes straight ahead. It was cold.

They'd driven the last ten minutes in silence until they pulled into the Dawson gym parking lot. Jackson buses were nowhere in sight; only a few cars were parked around the lot. Marsh always arrived in plenty of time to see the warmups. Even though his leaving so early made it even harder for her to get away from the office for the out-of-town games, Erin had had little to say about it. His last-minute tips to Randi about what they'd better watch for with regard to the opponents warming up on the other end of the court were an expected ritual. Tonight was no exception. Forty-five minutes until game time.

"You want to go in?" Marsh asked.

"No. Those bleachers get hard enough by

half-time. Can't we just sit out here a while?"

"Okay." Then, "You're going to get cold."

"I've got a remedy for that." Erin scooted over closer to her husband and kissed him softly on the cheek before she could talk herself out of it. Marsh turned and pulled her to him. They sat for a few minutes, Erin resting her head in the crook of his arm. Then abruptly she slid backward on the seat away from him, slipped her shoes off, and plopped her feet up in his lap.

"So that's it." He began to massage her feet.

Erin sighed and moaned, ooed and ahed. "That feels terrific. You haven't lost your touch."

Marsh clasped her toes in his hands and bent them forward, then backward, then turned them round and round. After a moment, he asked. "Did you think I would?"

"Would what?"

"Lose my touch?"

Erin smiled and shook her head. Tears came into her eyes and she didn't understand why.

The buses were now pulling into the parking lot, and the other parents' cars behind them. Marsh pulled her close to him once again and kissed her before they got out of the car to follow the crowd inside.

"Hi. Hello. How are you?" Groups of parents greeted each other.

"You haven't met my wife, have you?" Marsh spoke to the Monroes, regulars at all the games. "This is my wife, Erin. Jerry and Sue Monroe."

They spoke and walked along toward the gym.

"Marsh is going to have to behave tonight, I guess," Jerry said.

"Oh?" Erin asked.

"Yeah. When you're not here he really makes a pest of himself with those referees."

"Now look out," Marsh said. "You're going to get me in trouble." He hugged Erin to him. "Embarrasses her. I can't holler when she's here."

"I promise to unmuzzle him then," Erin laughed, "because we sure do need this win."

"Marsh, don't let 'em dampen your spirits," Sue spoke up. "We need you. Somebody's got to keep 'em straight."

"But don't worry, Erin. He usually has some good-looking woman near enough to keep an eye on him," Jerry guffawed.

"Oh, I'm sure he does." Erin smiled and they walked on into the now well-lit gym. Erin followed along in their direction, assuming Marsh would want to take a seat with them; Marsh steered her further down the bleachers to an empty area away from the few fans who'd already taken seats.

"Who's going to be the life of the party if you sit down here?"

"They'll manage. I want you to myself tonight."

They took a seat about half way up the bleachers. Marsh spouted out statistics from the last few games as each of the Jackson girls pulled off her warmup suit and took the court for drills. Erin listened politely, not really caring about anyone's rebound attempts but Randi's. Marsh seemed to know the extent of each player's past injuries, how much the injury had affected her game, how many practices they'd missed for detention hall, which ones were close to breaking a district or state record. Obviously, he and Randi had spent more time discussing the game than she was aware of.

With less than ten minutes before game time, the Jackson side of the gymnasium looked deserted; a mere twenty or thirty people dotted the bleachers.

"It's got to be the weather," Marsh remarked. "Strictly too many fair-weather fans."

Erin smiled. "That's the first time I can ever remember anyone's using the cliche in the appropriate context."

"Stick around me and you'll get a review of all Bartlett's quotes."

There was a pause.

"It really makes me angry though," he said.

"What does?"

"People not coming, supporting them when they have a bad season."

A tall, dark-complexioned man in a turtle neck sweater and herringbone blazer started up the bleacher aisle. He paused in the aisle and smiled broadly. "Well, Erin. How are you? Bending gave you a weekend off for good behavior?"

"It was about time, don't you think? . . . Are you still collecting that collateral?"

"Sure, sure."

"Jack, you haven't met my husband, Marsh. Jack Turner."

They nodded at each other and shook hands.

"You've got a girl playing?" The man directed his attention more to Erin than her husband.

"Yes. Randi. Over there, number 14." Erin pointed to the end of the rebound line. The girls popped up like mechanized mannequins and batted the ball against the board in perfect rhythm.

"Well, I didn't know she was yours. I've seen her name in the papers, I think, but I just didn't put you two together." The man shrugged. "And, of course, I don't get to many games. There's always somebody wanting something."

"I know the feeling. . . . You have a daughter playing?"

"No, my niece. Kelly Pierce. She's been after me all season to come see her play. You'd think I'd pick a better night than this, wouldn't you?"

There was a pause in the conversation.

"What do you do Marsh?" the man asked.

"I'm with Memorial Hospital." Marsh stood up.

"Oh, tripping over all that construction, huh?"

Marsh smiled faintly.

"When's the completion date on that wing?"

"Late July, I think." Then, "Would you excuse me, please?" He climbed down the bleachers and stood at the railing a few moments. Leaning forward, he rested his elbows on the wooden bar, studying the court.

Erin and Jack Turner continued to chat a few minutes longer, he still standing in the aisle, Erin seated next to him. A few minutes later after Turner took a seat alone farther up the bleachers, Marsh returned.

"Who was he?"

"Citizens Bank. President."

"I didn't know bank presidents came to high school games. With all their pressing business and civic responsibilities. Marsh looked straight ahead as he spoke, already aware of how his sarcasm would affect Erin. The new hospital wing and the new chaplain's office, which never materialized in the plans, was something she didn't want to get into tonight. Or, maybe that wasn't it at all. Why did he always feel like he was competing with every businessman in town? Erin let the matter drop, straightened her back, directed her attention to the court.

"There's Michael," Marsh nudged her. "He and his buddies just came in."

Erin watched the three boys line up at the concession booth near the door.

"That hat!" Erin shook her head at the western hat he always wore perched far toward the front of his head, the brim making his eyes all but invisible.

"What're you grinning at?" Marsh asked.

"That outfit. You'd think he was straight in from milking the cows."

"Well, everybody can't dress like your banker there, can they?"

Erin didn't answer.

Mike and his friends climbed toward them, boots clicking the hollow bleachers with every step.

"Hey, Mike," Erin spoke as he was about to pass.

"Oh, hi, Mrs. Tilland, Mr. Tilland. I didn't see you. How you doing?" Mike stopped and shook hands with Marsh as his two friends walked on past and took a seat farther down the row.

"Not much, Michael. Yourself?" Marsh asked.

"Ah, not much." Then, "I guess I'll meet the bus and bring Randi on home, if that's okay? I already told her I would."

"Okay. But you better be careful; there's still an icy patch or two on the roads."

"Yeah, we will. . . . Well, see you later then."

"Okay, Mike," Erin said, and the young cowboy climbed on up the bleachers to join his friends.

Erin turned to Marsh, "Why do you always call him Michael?"

"No reason."

"Randi always calls him Mike."

"So?"

"So nothing. I just wondered."

Erin turned back to the court swarming with players and feigned interest in the drills. Yet thoughts of Randi's involvement in the game and the chances of injury consumed her mind. A cold shiver went up her spine as she watched the green-suited girls running, passing, dribbling, shooting baskets.

Why Randi out of so many? Was God punishing her for not doing something about the reports? She already knew what Marsh's answer would be, though she couldn't discuss it with him. No, he'd say, God didn't cause these things. Man brings his own corruption by his own free choice and his failure to take care of the environment. They'd had such philosophical and theological discussions often, especially during college days. The answers didn't satisfy now. Why Randi?

The preliminaries over, the players took the court in earnest. Randi played center forward; Erin's focus narrowed to that position. She watched every move, ready to spring from her seat.

The game proceeded from one end of the court to the other. Neither Marsh nor Erin talked much except to answer nearby parents' comments about a play or referee's call.

"Let's get her a car for her birthday," Marsh said to Erin during half time.

"She doesn't even have a license."

"She can take driver's ed next year and get her license early."

"But . . . ," Erin paused, "you want to get it now?"

"Start looking, at least. I don't want to get her just any old junk heap. It may be the only car. . . ." Marsh looked away. His statement was the nearest he'd come to discussing his feelings about Randi's illness since that first night.

"With a new car sitting in the driveway before she's even got a license, she'll be asking questions."

He didn't respond.

"Marsh, . . . we need to tell her."

"We've already discussed that." He kept his eyes on the empty court in front of them.

"No, we haven't discussed it. That first night we were too . . . emotional to think rationally. Anyway, she's in remission. You agreed that we'd tell her when she got in remission." Silence. "Marsh?"

He stood up abruptly. "I'm going to get coffee. Do you want some?"

Erin nodded, and he was gone. She watched him leave the stands and join the waiting line at the concession booth. Jerry Monroe stepped in line behind him and struck up a conversation. Even from where she sat, Erin could see the transformation in her husband's demeanor. The tight lines around his mouth relaxed; his chin tilted slightly upward. After a moment, his gestures became more animated and he laughed heartily. Dying within, vibrant without. She remembered the night she'd been reading the newspaper and had come across an article discussing the fact that over ninety percent of parents who'd lost a child developed marital difficulties. She'd not shown him the article but had fought against the idea in her private world. Why couldn't they share what was happening to them, what they were going through? If he would just remove his mask with her.

As the game resumed, Marsh returned with the coffee and directed his attention to the court without any indication that he remembered the interrupted conversation.

Why couldn't she pretend like he was doing? Certainly she had more reason. Six times more likely. She could see the words on the page even now. Yet she had stayed.

Erin's head ached, but she could not take her eyes off the court. She followed her daughter's every move, every reaction, every dribble, every shot. Randi's arms went into the air, her feet pivoted. She bent low and swung around coming up under her guard's arm to try to get the foul shot. Every stumble, every shove, every charge, every tie-up, every jump, every rebound offered new danger.

Erin turned away. How could she tell her she couldn't play on the team because her mother couldn't take the wear and tear? This same mother who'd carried the knowledge that she was living in a dangerous radiation zone. What right did she have now to speak up, to cry out, to tell them what she'd done. How unthinkable to ask her daughter not to take the risks, not to live with the consequences of her mother's decision! She had stayed.

The final buzzer sounded.

Six

Finding a hole in the steady stream of traffic from the airport terminal, Erin pulled into an empty parking slot. Inside the terminal, people darted from counter to counter, ramming each other with luggage and briefcases. Which way to the snack bar? She felt disoriented every time she entered the building from a different direction. An Avis Rent-a-Car sign struck a familiar note; she headed for the corridor to her left.

Gloria, who already had a table, caught her attention with a quick wave. Erin had no trouble spotting her friend's bright melon tunic and bangling bracelets. She always stood out in a sea of drabness.

"I got here just in time to get the only table left," Gloria said when Erin approached.

"Am I late?"

"No, I'm four minutes early."

Both women smiled at their private joke. Gloria had sent a note home with Randi which said parents must pick up their children promptly after piano lessons. Randi had read the note in front of her new music teacher and announced, "My mom's never been late in her life." Two weeks later when Erin had phoned to ask about paying for the lessons with one check several months in advance, she'd failed to identify herself. Gloria responded that she must be the mother "who'd never been late in her life." They'd laughed over Randi's characterization and found their first common trait.

Erin took a seat facing the window. "I feel like I'm in the wrong terminal. I didn't know Jackson had this many people."

"Just on the weekends. They all leave Monday. You're the statistics nut. How many people fly out of here every week?"

"Not exactly my category, but I've probably clipped an article about it somewhere."

"Sorry about having to ask you to come out here. But there wasn't any other way to cram lunch into what I had to get done this morning."

"Oh, no problem. In comparison to the company cafeteria, this is exotic. Next time I'll give you more notice."

Both women studied the menu and ordered salads.

"It won't take long, will it?" Gloria asked the waitress. "I've got to catch a flight at 1:20." The waitress assured her the salads would be right out.

She turned back to Erin. "I'm so glad you

phoned and finally caught me in town."

"Well, that is a feat, you know. Where are you headed this week?"

"Atlanta. My boss's considering setting up a branch office there. I've got a list of preliminaries I'm supposed to check out for him before he makes the trip himself."

"Hmmm." Erin nodded. "You're still enjoying your job then."

"Love it. Love it." She squealed, bracelets jangling as she gestured. "It's mostly traveling right now. Since I'm single, I think they throw all the trips my way. But I'm not complaining. In fact, I told them I'd be willing to make all the trips necessary."

"Well, you look like it agrees with you. But that much traveling wouldn't suit me."

"You've got a family. That makes a difference."

"I guess."

Erin was thrilled to see Gloria so radiant about the job. She'd been instrumental in getting her the interview with Rowan. In fact, she'd encouraged her friend's new career choice. When Randi had begun lessons over five years ago, Gloria was clearly undecided about what she wanted to do. Having recently graduated with a music degree and failing to find a teaching position, she'd opted for teaching private lessons. Then bored being home so much of the time, she'd wanted more opportunity to relate to adults. And, too, Erin and she, despite their mutual interest in music, had discussed the limitations of that as a career choice, especially in a place like Jackson. Gloria had toyed with the idea of beginning a master's program; Erin had suggested the business administration field. Two years later, Gloria had her degree.

"Say, tell me how you are?"

"Okay."

"Really."

"Better."

"And Randi?"

"Great. Everything's back to normal. Whatever that is. I can't believe sometimes how normal it really has been. You'd think with something like that," Erin paused while the waitress delivered their food, "that somehow everything would take on a monumental change. It doesn't."

Gloria took a long sip and gazed into Erin's face. "She's still in remission, isn't she?"

"Yes."

"Doesn't she have to go in for some kind of treatments?"

"No. She's on a maintenance program—a drug taken orally—to help her maintain the remission. Then she goes in every six weeks for a bone marrow test."

"Can she do anything she wants?"

"Can and does."

Erin related the statistics of the basketball season. Her scores, field goals and free throws, for each game. Gloria looked impressed.

"Well, sounds like she's adjusted fine. And you?"

Erin nodded. Details about the illness, which she hadn't been able to share with anyone, Marsh included, tumbled out. There was a short silence; Erin checked herself. She hadn't intended to monopolize the conversation with all this. "Did you say you were going to Atlanta?"

"Yes."

"That's where my folks live. You ought to give them a call and say hello while you're there."

"I will. Give me the number," Gloria answered. "And I mean it. I'm not one of those persons who's always saying I'll call somebody some time and then never gets around to it. I really do it."

"Well, good." Erin put down her fork, pulled out a card from her purse, and wrote her parents' phone number on the back.

"Do they know about Randi?"

"Yes. I called them the same day I called you, in fact. They wanted to come out here, but I discouraged them. They're older—late sixties. Daddy hates to fly. And I told them an unexpected trip so soon after Randi's hospital stay—more than their once-a-year summertime trek—might arouse Randi's suspicion."

Gloria nodded and tucked the card into her billfold.

"She still doesn't know?"

Erin shook her head. "Marsh still says no."

"Are you sure you're doing the right thing? I mean I'm not trying to pry or anything, but . . ."

"No, I'm not sure. I'm very unsure."

"Don't you have a say about it?"

"Marsh is the psychologist."

"But that isn't even the commonly accepted way to handle it now, is it? I thought doctors nowadays told patients."

Erin shrugged. "If I insisted, I guess he'd agree. I guess I'm a little afraid that I might be wrong. That Randi really couldn't take it."

"How about Marsh's parents? Do they know?"

"No. He didn't want to tell them."

Gloria waited for more explanation. Erin took another bite. She'd never really discussed Marsh with anyone, felt it somewhat disloyal. Gloria was still looking at her inquisitively. "He's not too close to his parents. I think because he feels like he's the blacksheep of the family."

"The blacksheep? A chaplain?"

"I guess every family labels their own members with a different system in mind. His younger brother, nine years younger, has always been their favorite. Marsh doesn't mention it much, but it's still obvious even to me when we're around them at Christmas or vacation. . . . His brother Matt was always sick when he was little. Asthma, really bad. Nearly died several times, I think. Their parents just gave over to him on everything, set their whole schedule around him. And Matt was what you'd call an over-achiever in school. Magna cum laude. I think it must have been his way of paying his parents back. Making them proud of him for all the trouble he'd caused them. And, of course, they were and are. Proud of him. He's a lawyer now for a big corporation, really raking in the money."

"And that makes Marsh the blacksheep?"

"Well, not exactly. Maybe I'm using the wrong word. Left out, maybe. His brother needed the extra attention when he was little, and theirs—Matt and his parents—was just a special relationship. I think Marsh just feels like he disappointed them. They wanted another doctor or lawyer."

"But telling them about Randi. What does that have to do with it?"

"I don't know. Another disappointment, hurt to them, I guess." Erin looked away, rummaged through her salad at length. "I'm glad my parents are coming out in August as usual. Randi always enjoys having them."

"Good." Gloria let the subject drop. She wrinkled up her nose. "This dressing tastes horrible, does yours?"

"A little rancid, now that you mention it."

"I kept thinking it was the deviled eggs. Maybe they'll use it up this month and make a new batch." Gloria continued to scrape the dressing from the larger pieces of lettuce.

They ate in silence for a few minutes. Erin had never really discussed her marriage relationship with Gloria. Except the relationship as it involved Randi. Because of Gloria's background in education, Erin had mentioned the gap between them in the hopes that maybe her daughter had confided, or at least conveyed through her attitudes, some of her feelings. But despite Gloria's rapport with her and her leading questions, Randi had never said much about how her mother and she got along. Erin had hinted at the part she felt Marsh had played in the relationship but had not gone into detail. So many times, Gloria had dumped her problems out for airing. But something held Erin back from similar disclosure.

Intimacy between women friends was a habit, Erin decided. One she'd lacked both time and motivation for in her earlier married life. Gloria's was the first close friendship she'd had in years, yet she'd almost let the relationship die through sheer neglect. Marsh would have approved of her keeping her mouth shut about their marriage. Whining women, he contended, complicate their own marriage problems and feed on each other's dissatisfactions. Maybe he was right.

They finished the salads with small talk about the details of Gloria's up-coming trip and new dating relationship. She'd finally met a man who could hold her attention more than two or three evenings. Erin was happy for her.

There was another long pause while the waitress cleared away the dishes. Time for Gloria to leave. Erin had not yet mentioned what was really on her mind.

"I'll tell Randi we had lunch today. She still mentions you occasionally."

"Good. She still like Mike?"

"Yes. And she's dating now. They're going strong."

Back on the subject of Randi. Why couldn't she bring it up? Maybe Gloria would say something else about the illness. Would she understand or blame her if she knew about the report?

Erin sighed audibly. She'd never really believed she could tell her. Wishful thinking. Gloria couldn't advise her about what to do, whether to tell Marsh, the press, who. She'd be irate herself if she knew about the government's role in the suppression of the research. That was a pet peeve of hers—the government's attitude about the public's right to know. Erin inwardly laughed at herself. Supervising twenty-three employees and asking an outsider what to do about her job. No, not the job so much. What to do about how Marsh and Randi would feel? She couldn't tell her; it was merely an illusion of freedom she didn't have.

"Well, listen. Enjoyed it. But I've got to run. My flight leaves in twenty minutes."

"Sure. . . . I'm glad we finally got together after so long."

"Me, too. Sorry about having to make it out here, though."

"No problem," Erin smiled. "The lettuce was still green."

Gloria screwed up the corner of her mouth and gathered up her tote bags. "One of these days we'll get out the tennis rackets and scout us up a teacher."

Erin nodded. That, too, was another subject of previous chats—the need for exercise and no initiative in learning the game. She'd never bothered to suggest Marsh as an instructor. She needed this relationship, however neglectful she'd been about it, to be her own. Just one person to talk to. She ached from sheer restlessness.

They paid their bill, and Erin walked Gloria to the metal detector. "Call me when you have another free minute," Erin said.

"Sure. You, too."

Gloria handed her purse and tote bags to the attendant and stepped through the frame. She was the last in line; the attendant whisked her through. Erin lingered a moment, watched Gloria half-walk, half-run down the corridor. Then she turned and headed toward the parking lot. Maybe when Gloria got back, they'd get together for a more leisurely lunch. She'd tell her about it then.

Later that evening, Erin mentioned the lunch to Randi.

"I saw a friend of yours today."

"Who?" Randi continued to do her algebra.

"Gloria Delacourte."

"Hmmm. What did she have to say?"

"She asked about you and Mike."

"What did you tell her?"

"That you were dating now, that he was keeping the road hot between here and Jackson."

"She should be glad. She liked him."

"She was leaving town for Atlanta. A business trip. I told her to call your grandparents while she was there."

Marsh looked up from the newspaper, caught Erin's eye.

"She will. Call, I mean," Randi said. "She really will."

"I know." Erin smiled.

Randi turned back to her homework. Erin wandered on into the living room to dust the plants. A chore she hated but performed regularly. Like the rest of the housework. She had asked Marsh once about hiring help; he'd said to go ahead if that's what she wanted to do. She'd changed her mind.

Why couldn't she just flop down in front of the TV, read a book, leave the carpets matted and the mirrors smeared? She knew why. No matter how meaningless, it filled the void. She sprayed and wiped the last leaf of the corn plant sitting at the end of the sofa.

Marsh appeared at the door. She saw him out of the corner of her eye.

"Did you tell her about Randi?" he said as he walked up behind her.

"I can't hear you."

Marsh repeated the question in the same hushed tone.

"She already knows. I told her right after we found out." She turned back to the plant.

He stood behind her, hands hanging on his hips, for a moment longer. She turned around and headed for the next plant. He stepped aside, let her pass. She continued to wipe leaves. When she turned around again, he was gone.

"She have any more piano students now?" Randi asked when she came back into the den a few minutes later.

"No. She's traveling too much with her new job to be tied down."

"Oh," Randi nodded. Then, "I'm kinda sorry I quit taking lessons now. I guess you were right."

Seven

On Friday night Erin arrived at Hayden's Department Store to find no sign of Randi. She parked in the usual corner of the parking lot near enough to the employee exit to see all the clerks as they went home at the nine o'clock quitting time.

The door continued to swing open. A lady with a red Afro hairdo came through. Behind her, a young black, his sports jacket flung over his shoulder, whistling. Still no Randi.

Erin shook her head; the inconvenience of having to pick her up far outweighed the extra spending money proposition Randi had jumped on. As soon as Randi had seen the store's ad for extra help during the Easter season, nothing could dissuade her that the job might not work into her already crowded schedule. It might or might not turn into something for the summer. The job, however, had been a contention between them only in

Erin's mind. Both she and Marsh had wanted her to be free to enjoy school activities and her friends while—the "while" was something they never put into words, even to each other. To do so would have cast doubt on their dream.

By the time her sixteenth birthday rolled around, Randi had been in remission two months and showed no signs of coming out. *Could hold her in remission for years*, the doctor's words kept coming back to Erin, comforting, reassuring. From the beginning, Erin had sensed Randi's need to be in control of her sickness and left her on her own as much as possible. Yet she couldn't break the habit of checking the medicine bottle periodically to see that the appropriate number of pills was missing.

The door stopped its periodic swinging open. Erin sat up taller over the steering wheel. Had they already locked up from the inside? She glanced at her watch. How long ago had it been since the last person had come out? And where was Randi?

Outwardly calm, she got out of the car and strolled up to the exit door to see if it was locked. As she approached, the manager came out with the key ring on his arm.

"Excuse me. I'm Erin Tilland. My daughter, Randi, works here." Erin paused, not sure he would recognize the name.

"Yes, Mrs. Tilland, what can I do for you?"

"I came to pick her up, and I haven't seen her come out yet. She still inside?"

"I don't know. I . . . really hadn't noticed. Where did she work tonight?"

"I didn't hear her say, but she's been in ladies-ready-to-wear the last couple of times."

"Just a minute." The rotund manager sallied over to the phone beside the time clock and dialed.

"She worked in that department all right," the manager announced, returning to where Erin stood. "But we sent her home about 7:00. Slow night. At least slower than we expected. The division head let her go."

"Oh, . . . I see."

"I'm sorry if that inconvenienced you." The manager scratched the back of his neck. "When we use kids like that . . . well, they don't always have their own transportation. Makes it hard, but . . ."

"I don't guess her division manager saw her leave with anybody?"

"No, she didn't mention it if she did. . . . I'm sorry." The manager looked duly concerned, still scratched the back of his neck. "Would you like to use the phone?"

Erin shook her head. "I don't know who to call." She took one last look around the time-clock area, the stockroom shelving and aisles full of boxes. "Thank you."

She turned and walked back out into the night. On the way back to her car, she gazed around the dimly-lit parking area but could see no sign of a familiar person or car which could explain Randi's absence.

She flitted through a list of possible attractions. Now that basketball season was over, Randi had filled her time with so many new activities and friends. Tennis. Spanish Club. The world belonged to her again; she wallowed in her freedom; Erin felt no such luxury.

The fears mounted. What if someone—a customer or employee—had seen her getting ready to leave and forced her out of the store? What if she'd fainted in the restroom or had a severe nosebleed, and the blood wouldn't clot? What could have lured her away from the store? Why hadn't she at least phoned? Where could she have gone without transportation?

She'd obviously gone off with someone. But who? As far as Erin knew, no one she ran around with worked anywhere near. Erin flitted through faces at Randi's recent birthday party. Remembering the party's success, she smiled at the conflicting image of herself as mother. She definitely had not been the worried, harried, over-protective mother where that was concerned. No holds barred, they'd had a good time. She and Marsh had offered to take her on a trip somewhere—a long weekend campout. But Randi had opted for a big party instead. She, Carrie, Mike, and Meganne had spent hours planning all the details from how to keep the food warm down to how to arrange the furniture to accommodate more people. It had met all Randi's expectations. Erin went through the guest list again remembering no particular new friend who might indicate a change of schedule, a new Friday night happening.

She pulled the car slowly around the parking lot, glancing from side to side looking, for what, she didn't know. What good would it do to tell them now that she was sorry she'd wanted to live here? That she was sorry they'd breathed contaminated air ten, fifteen years ago?

Why had they let her start working anyway? Why not, Randi would ask. She wasn't sick anymore. How could they convince her that there were more important things than making spending money to buy a car? Certainly, she didn't feel any need to work to buy extra clothes or such. They'd always taken great care never to discuss finances in front of her. Their fears about the money needed for medical bills had been unfounded so far. With two good insurance policies and Randi's quickly achieved remission, the expenses had been moderate. Quietly they had increased the percentage of their savings each month to cover future bills. Both were determined Randi would never hear medical bills mentioned. No, Randi's working was definitely her own idea, for her own satisfaction.

But work had been good for her, Erin couldn't deny that. Although her parents had never let her work when she was in high school, Erin could see the value in Randi's having a job. Self-discipline, for one. The discipline of working when more important things like unexpected invitations popped up. Randi grew furious when other part-time clerks who wanted the day off called in sick.

And then there were the telephone calls. Randi, with a mixture of pain and embarrassment for her division manager, had told her and Marsh about them one night at dinner. She had answered the phone several times when what she assumed was a customer had asked to speak to her department manager, Mrs. Grisham. After answering, Mrs. Grisham had always lowered her voice and tried to step around the corner out of earshot. Randi, taking the hint, had busied herself and moved away from the phone. One particular day after she'd answered three or four such calls, Mrs. Grisham had confided to Randi that the calls were from a woman who was seeing her husband and was hounding her to give him a divorce. The calls came day and night. When Randi retold the information to her and Marsh later that evening, it was evident that the revelation had upset her. Erin, then as now, continued to reevaluate the working issue. Maybe that's why Randi was missing now. She and Marsh had kept her so cooped up, protected, innocent all her life.

Erin drove the length of the parking lot again, near the building entrances checking for shadows. Had Randi really suffered because she was an only child? She had clipped all the magazine articles and dog-eared all the pop-psychology books about the facts surrounding only children. Being an only child herself, she had never felt that she'd suffered any for the situation. In fact, statistics assured her that the most successful adults were the only or oldest child of the family.

Should she drive around town? Go by the school? But there was nothing going on there tonight or Randi would have lamented missing it. She pulled across another lane of parking space. A truck similar to Mike's caught her attention. She drove closer. No, the familiar decal on the back was missing. The Pilgrim's Cleaners sign flashed its message from across the street. She pulled into the service station across the highway and called home.

"Marsh, Randi's not at the store."

"Yeah. She called just after you left."

"Where in the world . . . what happened?"

"She's at Meganne's. She got off early."

"How did she get there?"

"Meganne was out at the store when they sent her home from work. They decided to shop around the mall for a while. She's . . ."

"Never mind. I'll be home in a few minutes and you can tell me." Erin hung up under the impatient glare of the station attendant.

Marsh lay stretched out on the floor watching television when she came in the back door.

"Now. What's the deal with Randi?" She banged the door closed behind her.

"She called a few minutes after you left to say she'd gotten off work early and that she and

Meganne had been walking around the mall."

"You know what time she got off?" Erin asked.

"No."

"Seven."

"Hmmm." Marsh shrugged. "Anyway, they ran into Carrie and all decided to go over to Meganne's. She's on the way home; Meganne's going to bring her."

"Why couldn't she call and let us know?"

"I don't know. I didn't ask her." Marsh reached up to turn the TV volume louder.

A car turned into the driveway. They heard laughter, a door slam, steps come up the sidewalk. They waited.

"Hi," Randi walked into the den. Her eyes, sheepishly downcast, betrayed her tone. She kept her back to them while she rummaged through her purse for something. Then, "These shoes sure do hurt my feet; I'm going to have to get me some of those stretchers." She stuck her finger in the side of her shoe and gouged around. "You think if I take them back to where I got 'em, they'd do it for me free?"

"Why didn't you call when you got off work?" Erin asked.

"I don't know. I just didn't. I thought I'd be home before you left to come pick me up."

"That's no reason. What do you think I felt like when I drove up to that door and you didn't come out?"

"I don't know." Randi looked in her dad's direction, but he still watched the TV screen.

She poked inside her other shoe. "This one doesn't need it, really. It's just the left one. Meganne said they'd do it if you still had the sales receipt. Do we?"

"Yes, we have the sales receipt." Erin paused. "I was worried to death. Afraid that you'd been forced to leave with somebody."

"Moth . . . errr. You always think something like that."

"I think you're old enough to remember to let us know where you're going. And you know you don't just go off with anyone somewhere without asking."

Silence.

"You remember where we got 'em?"

"Are you listening to what I'm saying?"

"Yes, I'm listening to what you're saying. I didn't call because I was afraid you wouldn't let me go."

"That's what I thought. You *could* have called if you'd wanted to."

"But you'd have told me to come on home."

"That's exactly right. A sixteen-year-old has no business out wandering around the mall alone at ten o'clock at night."

"Moth . . . errr, there's people all around."

"Sure there are, but that doesn't mean much. And that's not the point. The point is you know you're supposed to call home and ask if you can go somewhere."

Randi didn't answer, but instead stood with one hand on her hip, a smirk across her face.

"We just may have to tighten up some

regulations around here, do a little grounding if you can't remember that."

Randi yanked off both shoes and started off down the hall toward her room. For the first time since the discussion began, Marsh turned around from the TV.

"A little hard on her, don't you think?"

"Hard on her?"

"Yes."

"No, I certainly don't."

"Well, I do. She's sixteen."

"If you'd been the one up there waiting on her, worrying what happened, you'd feel a little differently."

Randi appeared in the doorway again.

"Come on, Erin. Give her a break."

Sure that Marsh had seen Randi standing in the doorway and had intended her to hear his last remark, Erin reddened.

"Where's the receipt?"

"In the middle drawer in my dresser."

Randi retreated again to her room. After her bedroom door closed, the discussion continued in lower tones.

"I don't see why you stay on her for something like that."

"Stay on her? I haven't been *on* her. I just think she ought to let us know where she is. She knows she's supposed to call."

"She said she forgot."

"No, she didn't. She was afraid I'd tell her she couldn't go to Meganne's."

"What's the difference anyway? She spent two

hours shopping; I don't see why you're so upset."

"I was worried, I told you. She could have been hurt somewhere."

"Well, I still think you went a little overboard. Grounding? How could you threaten to ground her knowing . . . what you know?"

"Just because she's sick doesn't mean we're supposed to let her get away with murder."

"With murder? Really, Erin," he hooted.

"You know what I'm talking about. She needs some guidelines the same now as always. We can't just forget about disciplining her."

"I didn't say anything about not disciplining her. . . . Look, you handle her your way; I'll handle her mine." Marsh turned back to the news program.

Eight

The only spot still raw and dead from winter's cold breath was the link between Erin and Marsh. The grass, luxuriously green from the melted snow, looked like a magnificent oil painting still wet to the touch. Was it possible these beautiful mountains still crowned with white and the fertile valleys between still harbored effects of the nuclear blasts long past? Erin never entertained the possibility for long.

Nevertheless, she felt a compulsion to bring the radiation research to light. Just as soon as Marsh would let her near him again emotionally, she intended to tell him, and the world for that matter, about the report tucked away in the file on her office shelf.

Maybe she'd call the *Daily Mirror*.

On Wednesday she came in late from work to find Randi, Mike, Carrie, and one unfamiliar body sprawled out on the den floor, accompanied by poster boards, magazines, library books, and magic-markers strewn from one end of the room to the other. Marsh was holding the newspaper in front of his face but obviously enjoying his ringside seat.

"Nobody invited me to the party," Erin said as she came to the doorway of the den.

"Oh, hi," Randi answered.

Erin greeted the first two faces that looked up but paused on the third.

"Vincent," the dark-headed friend sitting Indian style in the center of the clutter introduced himself.

"Creating a new design for the Sistine Chapel?" she asked.

"History project," Carrie answered.

"You all have history together?"

"No. Not in the same class. But we all—except Vince—have Ladimer. He always gives all his classes the same stupid assignments."

"Oh, I see."

Erin sat the small bag of groceries down on the counter and began to put things in the pantry. The kids' conversation, intermingled with Vincent's rendition of "Chop Sticks" on the piano, floated in to her as she started dinner. Not sure if they were intending to stay to eat, she decided on a larger casserole than planned.

Shoving it into the oven, she sauntered back through the den into the bedroom. Marsh followed.

"Tired?" he asked and closed the bedroom door behind him.

"Yes. They bogged down in accounting, and

I had to send my two temporaries over to help out. Now we're behind schedule again."

She sat down on the bed and took off her shoes. He stood in the center of the room, watched her. Her lips were still coral, the glossy shine gone. The hollow of her cheeks, a little deeper.

"How long have the kids been over here?" she asked.

"Not long I don't think. I just got home myself half an hour ago."

She began unbuttoning her blouse.

"Need some help with that?" Marsh pulled her up to him and kissed her. He began unbuttoning her blouse; she dropped her arms and let him fumble with the buttons.

"Nothing like a little relaxation at the end of a hard day. Isn't that what I always say?"

"I think I'm two notches past exhaustion."

"You don't look it. You're beautiful. Did anyone tell you that today?"

"Oh, a couple dozen."

He lifted her short, dark hair back and kissed her on the earlobe. She slowly stepped out of her skirt and slip between his kisses and caresses. She stood for a moment leaning against him, relaxed into his embrace. Then she pulled away and reached into the closet for her kimono. When she turned around, he eased her onto the bed.

"The kids are in there."

"So?"

"And the casserole's already in the oven; it

just needs to heat a few minutes."

He pressed his lips over hers for answer. She responded. They made love.

Without a word, she got up and went into the bathroom. A sadness enveloped her, squeezed her. Tears filled her eyes. Always spur of the moment now, their lovemaking. Arouse, indulge, before there was time to think, to recall harsh words, angry looks, selfish actions. But each time the occasion arose, her body fought her mind and won. It was all wrong. Not how it should be, not how it used to be. But at least it could be a road back together for them. She wanted to hang on, widen the lanes. The sadness permeated her entire being.

After a long time, she opened the bathroom door and walked out. Already dressed, Marsh sat on the bed holding her kimono open for her. Neither spoke. She dressed and left the room.

"Not there, dummy. You're gluing it on upside down. Quit flirting with Carrie and pay attention," Randi scolded Mike as Erin passed through the den and into the kitchen to check on the food.

"That's the top?"

"Yeah."

"Here, how does this look, Vince?"

"Don't ask me. It's not my project."

"You've still got an opinion."

"No, I don't."

Marsh walked back into the room.

"Daddy, look here. How does this look? Can you read it from there?"

"I can see it if that's what you mean. Reading your handwriting is going to be the problem."

"Ooooh."

"Here, Carrie. Go ahead and glue it." She threw the bottle of glue to her girlfriend.

"I'm not going to glue it." Carrie caught the bottle as it sailed across the room. "I always get it lumpy."

"You do it, Mike," Carrie tossed the glue to Mike on the other side of the room.

Randi raised from her squatting position just in time to get hit by the bottle in the face.

"Oh, . . . " she moaned, grabbing her nose.

"I'm bleeding." Randi, still kneeling, held her head back and tried to catch the flow in her hands.

Erin rushed from the kitchen, but Marsh was already bent over her, pulling her forehead.

"Lean forward. Forward, Randi," Marsh pulled her head down.

The three friends stepped back now, not sure what was going on.

"Hold her nose together. Pinch her nostrils," Erin gestured while Marsh pushed Randi's head further down between her legs. Blood continued to stream.

Erin reached around Randi's left side and pinched her nostrils together. "Like this. Now, just relax. Try to relax."

"Here," Carrie held out a wad of paper towels.

Erin took the towels and tried to wipe off Randi's shirt and arms with one hand while holding her nose with the other.

"I feel terrible," Carrie was saying over and over, but neither Marsh nor Erin heard her.

Erin still knelt poised on one side of Randi, holding her nose; Marsh knelt on the other side watching for results. Erin had little experience with nosebleeds, but two days following the doctor's mention of the danger of such an injury, she'd stopped by the library to check the proper technique in a medical book.

Randi sputtered and swallowed hard.

"It's going down my throat." She gagged. "I feel like I'm . . . gonna choke."

"Let's go. Get her in the car," Marsh said.

They lifted Randi to her feet, Marsh still holding her head forward as they started out the back door. All three kids followed them out, then stopped.

"Is there room?" Mike asked.

"Yes. Get in the back," Erin answered. Marsh and she maneuvered Randi into the front seat between them. Marsh whipped out of the driveway and headed for Jackson.

It was too crowded. Erin tried to move Randi around to get her head still lower between her knees.

"Is it still bleeding?"

"Some."

They rode along in silence, all eyes on Randi. Erin brushed her daughter's hair back from her face with one hand while holding the discarded bloody towels with the other. Randi scratched at the bloodstains on the front of her shirt and jeans.

The emergency entrance buzzer immediately brought nurses to escort them to the examining room. Carrie, Mike, and Vincent took seats in the nearby lobby, while a third nurse handed Marsh a clipboard and form to fill out. He passed it on to Erin and followed Randi's procession past the swinging doors.

"I can't believe it," Mike said.

"I've never seen a nosebleed like that."

"Me either."

"I didn't think I even threw it that hard. I just tossed it normal like. I feel terrible."

"It's okay," Erin said absent-mindedly to the last remark directed to her. Address, family doctor, office number, insurance number. She read the questions aloud to herself to try to force concentration. She finished the form just as Marsh returned and took a seat across the room.

"I told them," he said to Erin. She nodded.

All five sat around the lobby, the three teens still discussing the incredibility of the injury, both parents silent.

The bouts of nausea, the bone-marrow tests—she had withstood it all. Not to mention the basketball games. Injured by a glue bottle. Erin could only shake her head.

The emergency entrance buzzer sounded again. The nurse behind the desk came through the waiting room to admit a tall, lanky man, about twenty-five. Showing the nurse the gash in the calf of his leg, he limped on in behind her through the swinging doors. All five sat listening to the muffled voice explaining how he received the cut.

"Should we call my parents or somebody to come get us?" Carrie asked. "I mean, you might have to stay here for a while and don't want us hanging around."

"Just wait. We'll see," Marsh answered her this time. Her whiny voice grated, irritated. She sat back down and leaned her long sun-streaked hair back against the wall.

A thin doctor, Adam's apple protruding, approached them. "Are you Randi's folks?"

"Yes," Erin and Marsh both answered and rose mechanically from their chairs.

"Come on back."

They followed him down the cold hallway into the treatment room where Randi lay on the examining table. She made no effort to turn toward them when they came in. She looked very pale, her entire face puffy, dried blood around her hairline.

"She'll be all right now." The doctor patted her knee. "Just a little scare there, huh?" Randi gave a slight nod.

He turned back to Erin and Marsh. "We've had to go in there with a nose pack. We went in through the mouth up behind the soft palate. The pack's in there tight, can't move. The front of the nose is packed, too. She's going to have some difficulty talking, though, until we get that out."

"But she's okay?" Marsh asked.

"She'll be fine. But we are going to keep her

for observation. Let her own doctor check on her in the morning."

"Is there a chance it'll start bleeding again?" Erin asked.

"It could. She'll be all right here, though, where we can keep an eye on her."

Erin and Marsh moved around to the foot of the examining table so Randi could see them without having to turn her head.

"The nurse'll be in in a minute to clean her up and get her into a room. We're a little short-handed around here tonight." The doctor smiled and left the room.

"Do you hurt?" Erin asked.

Randi nodded again ever so slightly. Both parents stood staring at her, at a loss for what to do. Marsh paced around the room a minute or two, read the signs about payment in advance for emergency services, the anti-smoking slogan from the American Cancer Society, a plaque containing the "Parent's Creed." Then he stepped out in the hall, looked around, and walked back into the examining room.

"Why don't you go on home? Take those kids. Their parents will be wondering where they are," Marsh said.

"Why don't you, and I'll stay?"

"Because . . . you've got dinner half started . . . and I don't know what to do with the food."

Erin looked at him incredulously, then wagged her head. "They're not in a hurry

. . . . I want to wait until they get her into a room."

Both parents stood in front of their daughter, refusing to comply with the other's suggestion. A petite nurse, who looked not much older than Randi, came in with a cotton ball and solution to clean the bloodstains from Randi's face, arms, and hair. After asking Erin and Marsh to step out, she helped her patient into the loose-flowing hospital gown, then ushered all three down the hall toward Randi's room.

"One of you'll need to go to Admittance," she said.

Marsh kept walking.

"Which way?" Erin finally asked, disoriented from having entered the building from the emergency wing.

"Down this hall to the elevators and then left."

Erin returned from Admittance to find Randi in bed. Marsh stood beside her holding her hand. The lines across his forehead, the clenched teeth frightened Erin. She paused in the doorway a moment. He was suffering more than Randi; Erin's anger at his leaving the admission details to her melted. She walked on in.

"Still hurt?" she asked.

"Here." Randi pointed to the bridge of her nose, then gestured toward her stomach. She was ghastly pale.

"Are you sick to your stomach?"

"Yes."

"That's because you swallowed so much blood. That's what that shot was for. Nausea," Marsh explained.

Both parents stood staring at their daughter, who looked so fragile against the white-clad bed. Randi closed her eyes. Healthy, vibrant, laughing, only a couple of hours earlier. How many more times would they stand over her in similar anxiety, Erin wondered.

She left to take the other three kids home. She would call the newspaper tomorrow.

Nine

"My car's gone!" The young nurse rushed into the nurse's lounge out of breath. "My car's gone; somebody's stolen my car," she repeated.

"Are you sure? Did you park it in a different place last night?" an older nurse responded. "I did that once. Couldn't for the life of me remember where I left it," she chuckled.

"No. I know where I parked. Right where I always do."

Marsh passed the lounge area in time to hear the last statement. He walked to the doorway and recognized Sandy. Steve, her intern husband, had come in once a few months earlier and casually mentioned that he and his wife were having marital problems. He had not mentioned it again or attempted to set up a definite counseling appointment since. Although Marsh and Sandy frequently ran into each other, she'd never mentioned any problem.

"What's the matter? Somebody hide your car?" he asked.

"No. It's gone," she insisted again.

"Can't find your car. So that's why they tie the medicine bottles to your wrist. That's what I call playing the dumb-blonde role to the hilt."

She pursed her lips. "I'm serious, Marsh. Somebody's stolen my car."

"Come on, let's go find it."

He ushered her out into the cool pre-dawn air.

"Right over there. That's where I parked, and it's not there."

"You were in the Chevy?"

"Observant, aren't you?"

"Extremely. I never forget a car."

"Well, you goofed. Steve's driving the Chevy. I'm in the Buick."

Marsh gazed around the fairly well-lighted lot and then walked through several aisles of parked cars out into the thru-street and back again. Sandy stood under the breezeway roof, hands in her pockets, shivering.

"I don't see it out here. You sure you didn't park on the other side?"

"I'm sure."

A light blue Chevy pulled into the parking space near the front side entrance. "That's Steve." Sandy headed toward her husband and gave him the news.

The intern got out of his car and looked the parking lot over for himself, shook his head, and then entered the hospital without a word. Marsh and Sandy followed.

"Steve?" Sandy asked timidly, brushing her hair back into place with her fingers, "what do you want me to do?"

"Did you leave the keys in it?" he snapped.

She held the keys up to him.

"Just go on home. I'll take care of it." He reached into his pocket and handed her his keys.

"What're you going to have to do?" she asked.

"Call the police."

"Well, I could do that if you're in a hurry."

"I said I'd do it."

Sandy stalked out of the hospital without another word.

Marsh kept in step with the intern as they headed toward the nurse's station. Steve seemed to remember the chaplain's presence only as they brushed against each other rounding the corner.

"Sorry," he said to Marsh.

"Sure. I . . . anything I can help you with?"

"My wife." Steve nodded his red head in the direction Sandy had taken.

"Not any better?"

The doctor shook his head shyly, a complete metamorphosis from the scene a few minutes earlier.

"Why don't you drop by later today? I'll be around whenever you have a few minutes."

"I may do that. About 1:00. Maybe the last session didn't take." Steve attempted a smile.

"Well, now, it does tend to take more than a session or two to get to the problem." Marsh slapped the intern on the shoulder. He was not aware the doctor had considered their earlier talk a "session." Both men headed on down the corridor in opposite directions to begin their day.

Marsh had been over to the clinic to check on Randi, who was feeling much better but was still swollen. He'd returned in time to make two patient calls and have lunch before Steve came by. If he came.

Marsh answered the light knock on his door to find both Steve and Sandy.

"I went home and couldn't sleep thinking about the car," she explained. "So I came back to see if I could catch Steve during lunch and he said he was coming by here and so . . . here we are," she finished in one breath.

Steve wasn't so casual about the appointment now that Sandy sat beside him on the couch. Both of them, obviously nervous, feigned relaxation. Steve draped his long, lean arm across the back of the sofa behind his petite wife. Sandy sat cross-legged leaning toward her husband.

"Glad you both decided to come. It's much easier that way." Marsh took out a pen and pad from his top drawer. "I hope you don't mind." He pointed to the tablet. "If I make a few notes to myself, keeps me from giving the same lousy advice twice." He smiled and then added, "By the way, what about the car?"

"I reported it to the police. They took the information. Said they'd be in touch if they turned up anything."

"Never think about things like that, do you? Getting your car stolen right from under your nose?"

"Never," Sandy replied.

The three continued to delineate the possibilities of catching car thieves and then to theorize how the job was carried off and why. After a few minutes, when both Steve and Sandy were at ease, Marsh got to the point.

"Well, tell me, how are things going between you two?"

"Hmmm," Sandy said; Steve didn't answer at all.

"You might start by mentioning what problems you each see in the relationship at the moment." Marsh directed his attention to Sandy.

"Well, if you're asking my opinion. . . ."

"I am," Marsh interrupted in a flippant tone. She smirked, then grinned before continuing.

"It's just that Steve's so irritable all the time. He's always complaining and nothing I do seems to make him happy anymore, you know? I'm on his nerves. Like this morning. You saw him. He acted as if I got the car stolen on purpose."

"Now wait a minute. I acted like I was upset

about the car. I never said anything about its being your fault."

"You implied it."

Her husband wagged his head.

"I'm not saying everything is his fault; it's just that I can't figure out what I'm doing. And all he does is gripe about every little thing that I know couldn't *really* be bugging him. I just think he could be a little more . . . appreciative." She toyed with a strain of hair, drug it through her teeth.

Steve made no response. Marsh scribbled a note or two, then looked up to Steve.

"How do you see the problem?"

"I'm a grouch; I admit it. But I can sum up the whole thing in a nutshell. We don't have time for each other anymore. She's coming to work when I'm getting home or the other way around. You saw how it was this morning." Marsh nodded. "It's like that all the time. Things are too busy."

"Well, it's not my fault," Sandy interrupted. "I don't want him to get on the quit-your-job-kick again."

"Oh, I see, you've already discussed them apples, huh?"

Steve continued, "I'm not on any kick. She's been working six years, and I haven't said a thing until now."

"How long have you been married?"

"Six years. She's been working since day one."

"Did you discuss this before you married—Sandy's working?"

"Sure we did. He said it was perfectly okay then—when we were desperate for the money. Now that we can get along, it's 'quit, we don't need it.'"

"Steve, how about it?" Marsh asked.

"I don't have a thing against her working. But I want to start a family, and I want her home when the kids come along."

"I'm not even pregnant yet!" Sandy glared at him.

Both Steve and Sandy looked at Marsh as if it were his time to draw conclusions and dispatch answers. Marsh scribbled a few more notes on his tablet, then leaned back in the rickety swivel chair and hunted for a comfortable spot.

"Once again, now, Steve, just what is it, exactly, that you have against Sandy's working?"

"Nothing. That's her terminology. All I'm saying is that I don't ever see her. . . . And if and when we have kids, I think she should be home with them. At least at the first. Don't you?"

"Wait a minute. I bet Marsh can state his own mind without coaching."

Marsh smiled. "It's not what I think that's going to change the situation. It's what you two think."

Sandy studied his expression a moment, looked from her husband to Marsh. Then,

"This is ridiculous. Why am I sitting here talking to you when you obviously agree with him?" The young nurse stalked out of the room as quickly as her short, high-heeled legs would move her.

Marsh looked abashed, glanced at Steve and then back again toward the door.

"Well, that's a first," Marsh said.

"Not for me. She pulls that stunt all the time."

Marsh forced a chuckle; it was an anxious laugh. Regaining his composure, he mimicked, "Well, you and me, Doc. What you say?"

"I say what's the use of trying? You'd think she was eighteen rather than a twenty-eight year old college graduate."

"This blasted chair is driving me crazy. Let's walk down and get something to drink."

Steve followed Marsh down the hallway where they got a couple of cokes and sat down at the corner table in the snack area. A rather elderly patient and his wife spoke to Marsh as they ambled past. The older woman stopped, took a few steps back toward the chaplain, and leaned over to whisper in his face. She smelled of Vicks coughdrops.

"Whatever you said to Eldon this morning sure perked him up."

"Oh? What was that?" Marsh asked.

The wife eyed her husband patiently waiting a few feet away, then turned back to Marsh. "He never said exactly. Just said you really hit home." She chuckled. "He even had the TV on when I came in at lunch. Hadn't watched it since he's been in here! I just praise the Lord."

"Good. I appreciate your telling me."

The woman bobbed her head in another approving nod, emitted another Vicks spray, and rejoined her husband.

"You always have to share the credit?" the intern asked.

"One of the hazards, or benefits, of the profession—depending on how you look at it, I guess."

"No, I really admire that. All that education, then choosing a profession that provides a one-to-one audience."

Marsh shrugged.

"We doctors get to play to a larger audience."

There was a long silence. The two men sat like strangers on a park bench. As in all relationships, Marsh drew a firm line between personal and professional matters.

He'd not always done so. He still remembered his attempt to confide in Doug Marlowe, one of the Baton Rouge hospital administrators who'd gone with him on an all-night fishing trip. Early one morning while frying bacon on the campfire, Doug had mentioned his recent divorce experience. Marsh had made a comment to the effect that Erin and he were having problems. The astonished expression on the administrator's face still cast a vivid image. There had been a few other occasions during counseling sessions when he'd grown especially close to a client and had attempted to mention something personal. Heavy silences and disbelieving expressions stopped him. Gradually Marsh had concluded that people expected a chaplain to have a firm handle on his own life. At other times, Marsh doubted these conclusions and judged his self-imposed silence a quirk of his own making.

"Your wife works, doesn't she?" Steve asked.

"You mean you don't know my wife?"

"Should I?"

"I thought everybody knew Erin." Marsh's tone was sarcastic.

Steve raised his eyebrows and waited for further explanation.

"She's head of the research department at Bending and Dowden."

"No, I don't think I know her."

Marsh shrugged and took another long swallow.

"But I do remember you have a Randi."

"Yes. Sixteen last month. You saw her picture in my office, didn't you?"

"Yes, I did. Pretty girl."

"She spent the night in the hospital last night."

"Oh?"

"A bad nosebleed. They had to pack it. Wanted to keep her for observation."

"Has she had trouble with nosebleeds before?"

"No." Despite the intern's inquisitive look, Marsh added nothing more.

There was another long silence while both sat surveying the surroundings. Vending machines lining three walls crowded the snack area; three sported "out of order" tags. The tables were all but deserted at this early afternoon hour.

"Well, . . ." Steve leaned back in his chair. "Surely I'm not the only husband left on the planet who wants his wife home with the kids?" His remark, more a question than a declaration, hung in the air. He tried again,

"I guess people pick up their parents' views naturally. I try not to do that. But my dad and mom's marriage—she never worked away from home—convinced me that that was the best way to make a marriage work."

Marsh nodded.

"I mean I know everybody's marriage has to accommodate their lifestyle to some extent. I'm talking about successful marriage, you know? The ideal. No. I'll qualify it—my ideal."

"A person can't help but grow up with parental prejudices. Especially marital ones. Role models. It takes a long time to overcome a parent's expectations. To live your own life."

"My parents have really given Sandy a hard time, I'll have to admit. She takes a guilt trip every time we go home for the weekend."

"Yeah, we all have to cope with other people's expectations and priorities. My parents just couldn't see a 'preacher' in the family. To them a theology degree meant preacher and preacher meant poverty and poverty translated into everything else they didn't want for a son. They pleaded, coaxed, and, when that didn't work, shamed me like first generation immigrants come to the promised land." Marsh paused and studied the grainline in the veneer table top. "But then that's maturity—refusing to let other people define you."

Steve nodded. Marsh finished tracing the grainline with the edge of his paper cup.

"You don't think your daughter has . . . missed anything then? With your wife's working?"

"Oh, no. . . . My wife's the type that wouldn't, couldn't be happy at home. No, she's always worked. Makes more money than I do." Marsh tilted his head to one side. "A man can't complain about that, can he?"

"Guess not."

"No, really I don't have anything against her working. That's just Erin. It's worked fine for us."

Steve's pocket pager beeped.

Marsh stood with the intern as he rose from the table. "Listen, drop back by any time you get a chance."

"Sure, thanks. . . . Just don't count on seeing Sandy again. She's not serious about it."

Marsh sat back down for a minute, then tossed his empty cup in the nearby wastebasket and walked back down the hall. Once inside, he stood in the center of the room staring at the volumes of books lining his wall.

The first time somebody ever walked out. The very first.

Ten

"Freda, would you dial the . . . never mind." Erin clicked the intercom off. She couldn't put her on the spot if and when people came around asking questions.

She called information and got the number herself. Dialing the second time, she listened to the faraway ring, then answer.

"Yes. I'd like to speak to the editor-in-chief, please."

"One moment."

"Mr. Logan's office. May I help you?" another secretary came on the line.

"I have some information I think your paper would be interested in."

"Let me connect you to one of our reporters."

"No, . . ." Erin caught the secretary before she clicked off the line. "No, I think this will need to go through the editor's office."

"May I ask who's calling, please?"

"I'd rather not say," Erin tried to answer as

congenially as possible under the circumstances. She recalled the rudeness, contempt she'd put up with during her days as secretary.

"One moment, please."

Waiting, Erin reopened the loose-leaf notebook on her desk, took out the folder, and again spread its contents before her. An almost daily ritual the last few months. She waited, poised, elbows resting on each arm of the chair.

She wasn't sure how to go about releasing such information. In fact, this was the first time she'd ever called the press. Usually reporters got wind of new studies being done by their firm elsewhere and then knocked on her door for verification.

She heard the early muffled morning clamor of the outer office. Far, faraway sounds. Sounds of another world. Time to hang up. Still time. The idea played in the back of her mind. Beyond her will. Her hand gripped the receiver tighter.

A man's voice came on the line. "Logan." His voice jarred; he sounded like gravel.

"I'm calling from Bending and Dowden Research. . . . I have a report that I think you'd be interested in."

"Oh?"

"The report's on a study done about ten years ago. A study showing a link between leukemia and radiation from nuclear testing sites."

"Ten years old, you say?"

"Yes. The government . . . nobody's seen the need to publish it yet, but I think the public would like the information."

"I see. Well, you know we've seen other studies along those lines published."

"Yes, I realize that. But this one is much more . . . ominous."

"I see. Who's calling, did you say?"

"I'd rather not give my name . . . over the phone. I'm with Bending and Dowden."

"In what capacity?"

"I'd rather not indicate that either."

There was a pause.

"All right. Would you like to meet somewhere?"

"Yes. I'd be willing to meet a reporter here in Jackson. Say at the Holiday Inn Coffee Shop."

"All right. I don't have a flight schedule handy, but let's see. . . . Monday morning at 10:00?"

"Okay."

"He'll be there at 10:00 sharp."

"Thank you." She hung up.

Freda looked up as Erin, carrying her purse, exited her office, closing the door behind her. The secretary glanced down at her watch. 11:00. Her boss rarely went out to lunch, but instead ate in the company cafeteria. An inquisitive expression spread over her face.

"How's Randi feeling these days? she called after her.

"Fine."

"Good. I hadn't heard you mention her lately. You look a little tired yourself."

Erin smiled tightly. "She did have a bad

nosebleed last night. They kept her overnight at the clinic for observation." Her throat felt tight. Keep moving, get out.

"A nosebleed? Must have been bad for them to keep her? That has something to do with the anemia?" Freda followed her toward the door, her baby-fine hair bobbing up and down.

"Yes. But she's all right. I stopped by on my way to work this morning. She's feeling much better."

"Good. Good. Must be convenient to have your husband work over there."

"No, he's at Memorial."

"Oh, how come I got that confused?"

Erin shook her head, slowly edged toward the door.

Freda boasted of almost twenty years with the firm. She more or less came with the job when Erin had taken over the department three years earlier. A congenial person, though not an outstanding secretary, she played Mother Confessor for the rest of the employees. She understood the corporate ladder, the sacrifice of relationships the climb required.

Though Erin rarely discussed personal matters, she preferred her secretary's prying to some other deficiency such as laziness or surliness.

Erin waited until she was almost out the front doors to add, "I won't be back today."

The parking lot attendant waved as she exited the lot. She failed to return the greeting. Her eyes cut out only her path between the white lines, and she drove oblivious to all other sights and sounds until out of the city limits.

At home, they key caught in the back door; it was almost as if the door were reluctant to admit this unexpected intruder in the middle of the day. She changed into jeans, shirt and low-heel shoes. Dressed, she left the house and again pulled back onto the main street through their housing area, then eased onto the highway. Slowly. Slowly. She had to drive slowly to keep the car in her command.

Eleven

Only when Hadley Lake came into view did Erin decide where she was going. She pulled the car off onto the one-lane gravel road. Under a shade tree on the edge of the lake, she turned off the ignition. As she opened the door to get out, the chilling breeze blowing off the water slapped her in the face. She slid back in the car and let the sunshine warm her through the windshield. As her muscles finally relaxed against the velour car seat, she felt free. Free from all eyes which might deprive her of her thoughts.

How was she going to tell Marsh? Would he understand that she'd never really believed it would happen? Her silence would be a personal insult to him. He'd never see his part in it, why she'd been hesitant to tell him. But who was she to determine what should go to the public? She didn't do it—bring the nuclear bombs and equipment into the area. What could she have done but tell him what'd already happened?

The sun continued to stream through the windows, warming her as she sat slumped in the car seat. A relaxing sensation rippled through her body, a release of unspent emotion. She began to cry. Without trying to hold back, she cried until the tears subsided. Then in the quietness of the midday, alone beside the deserted lake, her thoughts took free rein.

She remembered Randi's tonsillectomy as if it were as near in the past as her last clinic visit. She'd been the one to take her daughter in to the doctor month after month with recurring sore throats. And she'd been the one to insist they take the tonsils out despite the doctor's hesitancy. Marsh had hinted—no, more than hinted to Randi—that her misery was due to her mother's decision to have the tonsillectomy. She'd been on the defensive trying to convince Randi, that, yes, she wanted her to have her tonsils out, but no, she hadn't made them rotten in the first place.

She had taken off work the day of the surgery to sit near the operating room in case of an emergency. But Randi woke up from the anesthetic still too drowsy to be cognizant of her presence. Marsh had been the one to insist she go back to work, that it was senseless for both of them to stay around and watch her sleep. She had followed his suggestion out of her sense of practicality and left the hospital only to hear of Randi's "disappointment," as Marsh had referred to it, when she returned later in the afternoon.

She'd spent the night in the hospital in case Randi awakened frightened but had left for work the next morning after Randi's breakfast. Marsh had insisted on taking the responsibility of staying with her or of checking on her throughout the day. Thus, he'd been the one to bring in the ice-cream cones to sustain her through the raw-throat period. He'd been the one to bring her coloring books and "ooo-and-aah" over every page's newly created masterpiece.

"Daddy, you make the baddest time of my life the funnest," the six-year-old had said to her dad, hugging him goodnight the first night home after the surgery. How could a small child appreciate someone's sleeping in a chair beside her bed? Marsh's omission of words to that effect hurt Erin at the time. As they did now upon remembrance.

Well, at least yesterday she hadn't yielded to his pressure to leave the emergency room and take the three kids home. But even though she'd stayed, he'd offered the sympathy; she'd filled out the forms.

She surveyed the turbulence of the water in front of her. The brisk breeze whipped the water against the rocky embankment in sporadic splashes. The water's color matched her mood. She tried to analyze her behavior. Analyzing, another habit acquired from Marsh. Maybe she'd driven to the lake in a subconscious effort to recapture missed opportunities on past outings.

Randi and Marsh both loved the water and came out to the lake often, she joining them when she could on weekends. But she wasn't the type to enjoy the salty, sandy grit plastered against her skin. She came to be with them, but she was always the audience, they, the players.

Erin remembered the times she'd spent reclined in a lawn chair at the lakeside, watching them and thanking God that Marsh was such a good father. Taking fatherhood seriously from the very beginning, he'd changed dirty diapers, wiped runny noses, rocked through long nights. She'd appreciated his help then. Praised him often. Just when the tide of praise had turned to envy, she couldn't pinpoint. She hated to admit the feeling. But maybe it was the most accurate assessment she'd made of the situation in a long time. Ironic, his being such a good father was one of the reasons she always shut away the idea of divorce.

The injustices Marsh had done to her brought burning tears to her eyes again. He never once within her earshot had called Randi's attention to something her mother had done—pointed out to a happy-go-lucky child that someone shopped for her clothes, cooked the food, brought home the wrapped presents ready to deliver when she arrived at a birthday friend's house.

Not once had Marsh pointed out any of this to their daughter.

Erin leaned her head back against the car headrest. Even their last vacation two years ago had been a point of contention. They'd decided to take Randi to Texas to see some historical sights around San Antonio, the Alamo and the old Spanish missions, to go to the Dallas-Fort Worth area and take in Six Flags Over Texas Amusement Park, to tour the Galveston-Houston area and see the NASA Space Center. Being a history buff, Randi had helped Marsh arrange the itinerary with careful detail and delight. Both Erin and Marsh had planned to take two weeks vacation; she would have to be back to work Monday, July 16, and Marsh, Wednesday, July 18. These days had been agreed upon.

But as soon as they got to Texas, Marsh began his good-guy versus bad-guy routine.

Erin could tell from the moment they saw the performance of *Texas* in Palo Duro Canyon what Marsh was going to suggest. They arrived in Amarillo late in the afternoon, got a motel room, and then headed on out to the Canyon a couple hours before the musical performance, not adequate time really to see and hike through the Canyon. During intermission of the production, Marsh said "I sure wish we could stick around here another day to do some hiking." He pointed up to a craggy climb. "That'd separate the man from the girls, wouldn't it?" Then he and Randi mentioned other soon-to-be-passed-up pleasures of the area.

"Don't you wish your mother didn't have to get back on the 16th? Another two days sure would be nice."

Then on to Six Flags. Marsh started in again when they were less than two hours into the amusement park. "There's no way we could ever see everything in a day."

Randi agreed. "Could we buy a two-day pass? They sell them cheaper."

Erin recognized the familiar strain of conversation. "It's up to your dad."

Her statement took Marsh by surprise. He stammered a minute or two. "Well, since we've already bought these passes, I hate to waste the money to go back and pay another full day's fare, . . . but we'll see."

Marsh was uncomfortable having to consider the pocketbook; Erin had always done that. The "we'll see" turned into "no." But again the idea was planted; we're leaving early because Mother is in a hurry to get back to work.

Then to San Antonio. They'd allotted two days for the area, and this proved to be Randi's favorite stop of the entire trip. They spent almost six hours touring the Alamo and surrounding curio shops, with Randi poring over every letter collection with questions innumerable. "Did Jim Bowie really write this? Look how Travis spelled public. How did they keep the paper from getting torn up with so many relatives handling it? Look at this knife, would you? How can you be sure they really have the real stuff? On and on *ad infinitum*.

It was easy to see that they could have spent a week in the San Antonio area alone, walking along the River Walk, eating in the riverside restaurants, shopping the Spanish markets. Amidst the shopping spree Randi had announced her intention to take Spanish the following year and to join the Spanish Club.

Then on the riverboat ride Marsh suggested, "What do you say we let your mother fly back without us, and we'll come on a couple of days later?"

"Marsh, I . . . you know I'd like to stay, but I really have to get back."

"Sure. That's what I said. We understand, don't we, Randi? That's just what I said. You fly back and we'll come a few days later."

"Could we, really?" Randi started in. "That'd give us time to go through those old missions. Carrie said to be sure and go through the Governor's Palace."

After the night's discussion away from Randi's earshot, they'd decided all would return as planned—by car on the 16th. Erin couldn't see spending the plane fare for only two extra days; Marsh was easily persuaded. Yet, the stigma remained. To Randi, Mother had been the thorn in the flesh the whole trip.

Marsh had teased, "good-naturedly" as he'd called it, all the way home that when one had a working Mom, some sacrifices had to be made. And wasn't Randi proud of a mom who was so successful and important that they couldn't run a business without her for more than two weeks at a time. And wasn't Randi proud that her "dear old dad" was such a nobody that his plans didn't affect anybody or anything.

The trip had been unpleasant.

Tears of anger and regret continued to well up periodically with each remembrance as Erin sat in the car by the rippling lake. So many things she could have said, should have done to counteract the image. But she'd let them pass for fear of further alienating Marsh. It had been her life-long habit to shun conflict—with her parents, on the job, with Marsh. But then, she was mature enough to rid herself of anger without his ever knowing. Wasn't she? Or maybe she should beat a pillow to pulp or yell at the top of her lungs on some deserted farm-road.

Maybe Marsh was right. Maybe she was selfish. Maybe the anger was self-contempt. After all, she didn't object to his taking Randi places when she was tied up and couldn't leave the office. Did she use him when she needed him, then resent the results?

No. She'd done her share of the chauffeuring. She'd left work at 3:15 every Wednesday to drive Randi to piano lessons and then worked late the next day to catch up. Erin clenched her fists on the steering wheel as she thought about Randi's last recital. Even that! Randi's recital was scheduled on a night when she'd had to be out of town, only a two-or-three-times-a-year occurrence. The same old pattern. She'd driven her to the lessons; Marsh had praised the performance.

But there were other times. She had depended on him too heavily to take responsibilities where Randi was concerned. Like to the doctor. She should have taken off that afternoon. . . . But he always seemed willing to drive her places—to take off work. Did he really resent it? Think she used him?

As the early afternoon sun continued to warm the earth, Erin got out of the car and strolled along the edge of the water. Stumbling over a rock in her path, she kicked it aside, then stooped over to examine it. A cluster of tiny circular impressions in the rock's surface caught her attention. She decided the rock resembled a cell slide diagram in a Biology I book. Everything, it seemed, reminded her of the hidden diseased cells in Randi's body. Their whole family relationship. Diseased.

Did she really want a divorce? That question hadn't surfaced to consciousness in a long time. She'd logically assembled her reasons against the idea long ago. She didn't believe in divorce. Having grown up in a deeply religious family, she'd embraced the marriage-forever ideal long before she'd met Marsh. But it was more than that. Randi needed him. She flipped through her previously composed, easily recalled mental list of marriage pro's. He was successful. Intelligent. A good lover. Outgoing. Personable. In fact, his easy manner with people had been the first attraction. She'd always thought herself shy, reserved. She'd hoped that finishing her education would give her the added confidence to open herself to others. It had helped, but a gregarious manner still proved to be an effort. "Basically a shy person," wasn't that the standard way celebrities described themselves in talk show interviews? When she'd mentioned being hesitant to present a new idea to her boss, Marsh had laughed at her. She envied and admired his confidence. Or at least his mask of confidence, if that's what it was.

No, she'd decided long ago that divorce wasn't the answer she wanted for them. Once she'd discarded that idea as an alternative, their relationship had improved. The good times still outweighed the bad. Didn't they?

It was the illness that had knocked them off course again. If they could just discuss it, could face it together, rather than apart. But Marsh wouldn't let her close to him. If he could just admit he needed her.

She tossed the rock aside and stood staring into the water. It was 2:00, an eternity since she'd phoned the newspaper earlier in the morning. She'd done the right thing, she knew it. The muscles in her face relaxed; the set in her jaw drooped. Maybe she'd go back by the hospital, stay until the doctor made his rounds. A whole afternoon with her daughter. It was a place to start.

Erin got back into the car and pulled back onto the highway. Nearing the cut-off to their sub-division, she made a sudden right-hand turn and headed toward the house. Toffee bars. Randi loved them. She could make some in a half hour to take along.

As she poured the batter into the pan and slipped it into the oven, the phone rang.

"Hello?"

"Erin," Marsh's voice answered. "Where in the world have you been?"

"I . . ."

"It doesn't matter. I've been trying to reach you all during noon. The clinic phoned. Randi's lost her remission."

Twelve

Randi lay stretched out on the top of the sheets staring up at the ceiling.

"How do you feel?" Erin asked.

"Okay." Randi talked much better; they'd removed the pack from her nose. "But they say I can't go home yet."

Erin noted her daughter's still puffy curve of the cheekbones. "Where's your dad?"

"I think down talking to the doctor. Why are you dressed like that?"

Erin looked down at her shirt and jeans as if examining them for the first time. "I . . . decided to take the afternoon off. Come by here."

"To stay with me? I'm not that sick."

"An afternoon off. As in r-e-s-t."

Randi shrugged.

"I'll be back in a few minutes."

Erin walked out into the hall and looked

toward the nurse's station just as Marsh rounded the corner at the far end.

"Have you talked to the doctor?"

"I just came from there."

"What did he say?"

"Exactly what I told you on the phone. She's out of remission." He snapped his fingers. "Just like that."

"Did the nosebleed cause it?"

"No. The other way around."

"What do you mean?"

"She had the nosebleed because she was coming out of remission."

"What are they going to do?"

"Give her some transfusions. Start her on another drug. What else?"

Erin ignored the angry tone; this time she knew the hostility was directed toward the invisible enemy that dared loom up again when they were beginning to adjust and dream that the remission could go on indefinitely.

"We have to get some donors," Marsh added almost as an afterthought.

"How many?"

"Twelve. By tomorrow."

"Tomorrow?"

Marsh nodded.

"What type?"

"It doesn't matter. Any type will replace what they use."

"People are going to want to know—when we ask for blood." She paused to search her husband's face. "We have to tell her, Marsh."

He looked directly into his wife's eyes as if they were blazing fire threatening to consume him.

"Not yet."

"But she'll ask questions. The transfusions. Don't you think she can look us in the face and see it written there?" She lowered her voice. "She knows something's wrong, . . . Marsh?"

"No."

"But hadn't you rather she find out from us than hear it from somewhere else?"

"Who do you think she'd hear it from? You haven't said anything to anyone, have you?"

"No. But when we contact donors, somebody's bound to say something."

He stared at the blank wall beside them. Nurses and aides passed by them on both sides. She stepped back against the wall. Marsh remained in the center of traffic. He turned to face her directly. His eyes penetrated, punished.

"Not yet."

He turned and headed for Randi's room. When they walked in, the nurses were already hooking up the bottle of blood to overhang Randi's bedside.

"Say, Daddy, when you get home, would you call Mike and tell him not to come by tonight."

"Sure, Baby, but you can't count on his following orders."

Randi attempted to smile. "I don't want him to get sick of hospitals."

"Sick of hospitals? This is only the second time you've been in."

"I know, . . . but I'm afraid it may not be the last."

Marsh directed his attention to the magazine cover lying on the side of the bed. "That blood's gonna do the trick. They'll have you feeling as good as new in a couple days."

He tossed the magazine aside and leaned over to peck her cheek. "What you've got to do is decide how you're going to spend your spare time in here. Met any goodlooking boys in here?"

She shook her head. "I don't feel like doing anything now. Holding up that magazine is about all the energy I've got."

"That'll change. That'll change, won't it, Erin?" Marsh glanced toward his wife.

Erin, standing at the foot of the bed, smiled and squeezed her daughter's foot. "Maybe I'll be the one to relay the message to Mike. I think I'll go home, change clothes, and come back up later to spend the night."

"You don't have to do that. I'll be okay."

"Of course I don't. But I'd like to. Would you mind?"

Randi shrugged. "If you want to. But I'm okay."

"Good. Then I'll see you in a little while."

Erin hurriedly left the hospital and drove home. Who could she call for blood? Gloria, for sure. If she was in town. Her mind flitted through the faces at the office. They certainly would be willing to give if they knew the situation. But being their supervisor, she felt odd about asking. How could they say no? She didn't want them to feel . . . coerced. Freda, Ralph, Gary, June. They'd be glad to do it.

Thinking of Freda brought Monday morning's meeting with the reporter to mind. All the well-worn thoughts of that situation came rushing over her again and again like a high tide going in and out. She struggled for equilibrium to plan for the evening.

Phoning Mike took first priority. That little she could do as Randi had requested. Six o'clock. Likely a good time to catch him home eating dinner. Toffee bars. She took the pan of batter she'd shoved in the refrigerator earlier and put it in the oven. Then she phoned.

Mike's deep, manly voice, a deceiver of his eighteen years, answered.

"Mike, this is Erin Tilland. Randi asked me to call you and say she didn't feel like having you come by tonight. She's not feeling well at all."

"You mean she's still in the hospital—to stay?"

"Yes. She'll have to stay a few more days."

"From a nosebleed?"

"Uh huh, but don't worry. She'll be feeling better in a day or two, and I'm sure she'll feel like having company."

"All right, I guess. I'd still like to see her."

"Thanks. I'll tell her that. Maybe she'll call you."

Erin changed clothes to return to the hospital. Then pulling out her address book, she dialed Freda.

"Well! What did you do on your afternoon off? That makes two in the last three years, doesn't it?" Then, "There's nothing wrong, I hope."

"Actually, there is."

"I thought so. Taking an afternoon off, I mean. And then leaving without saying where you were going."

Erin left the morning's episode unexplained. "I hate to bother you at home, but I need a favor."

"Sure. What?"

"Randi's blood count is low again, and she's going to need quite a bit of blood. I was wondering if maybe you could donate some for her tomorrow?"

"Why sure. I'll be glad to. I'm so sorry to hear about that. I knew it must have been something like that. When you just walked out this morning looking so worried."

Again Erin let her secretary jump to the wrong conclusions. "Thanks. I'd really appreciate it. She's going to have to have twelve donors by tomorrow."

"Well, I'd be happy to," Freda repeated again. "Just don't worry about that. And I'm sure you're not going to have any trouble getting enough people. I'll pass the word."

"Thanks." Erin hung up.

Who else? Her work was the only place she'd thought of calling for donors. Then, Marsh's friends at the hospital? Who could he call? He seldom spoke of his associates. She didn't know who he was close enough to to ask.

Church came to mind. Although, they weren't closely aligned with any church because Marsh always worked on Sundays. The hospital administrators insisted that Sunday was the most crucial day for him to be present—that patients needed more emotional support when their doctors were hard to find. So Marsh's days off rotated during the Monday–Friday week. Randi's and her church involvement was limited to their Sunday morning attendance at the large Presbyterian church downtown where they knew few other people.

Twelve donors. She decided to call anyway. First thing tomorrow, she'd leave word in the church office. Better to ask people she hardly knew than to make employees uncomfortable about asking. She felt no longer capable of rational thought.

Erin got up from the bedside and began to pack a bag for herself for overnight and for

Randi, extra gowns and pajamas. She hated the blue and green ones the hospital issued. They were scratchy and the ties down the back poked her when she lay down.

Maybe she shouldn't spend the night. What if Randi should ask her what was wrong? She couldn't lie to her. Maybe she'd stay home and tell Marsh about the reporter when he came in. Get it over with. She certainly had to tell him before the story came out linking their company with the findings. Why had she dragged it out so long? She should have told him immediately after Randi was diagnosed. And he'd remind her of the lag, wouldn't understand why she'd waited.

Erin locked the back door and got in the car. She'd promised Randi she'd be back. The revelation to Marsh could wait. At least another day or two until after she talked to the reporter.

"Anybody home?" Erin walked into Randi's hospital room. Both Randi and Marsh watched the television set suspended from the ceiling. Already the transfusions had flushed her cheeks with color.

Randi spoke to her mother as she came in. Marsh glanced up, nodded, and then turned back to the movie. He looked relaxed, both legs propped up on the ledge in front of him.

Erin looked around for a place to deposit her overnight bag and hang her dress. Shuffling around the room, she unpacked Randi's things and put them away. She'd brought enough changes to last several days—until they could get Randi's blood count up and her new dosage regulated.

"Here." Erin set the box of toffee bars on the bedside table.

"What's that?" Randi asked.

"Toffee bars."

"Hmmm. Thanks." She reached for two.

Erin picked up the box and held it out to Marsh.

"You want some?"

"What?"

"Toffee bars."

He took several.

Randi and Marsh continued to watch the movie. Erin turned the straight-back chair around to face the same direction. It was a detective show. After a few minutes, she grew restless. Her mind could not be content to concentrate on some inane movie plot. Picking up the Gideon Bible lying on the window sill, she leafed through it looking for a familiar passage to read. She noted the page subject headings as she thumbed through. "Mary and Martha." Their situation exactly. She played Martha; Marsh played Mary. "Mary hath chosen the better part." She read the line several times before turning the page. After flipping through a few more pages, she closed the Bible. She sat in a daze trying to recapture the mood of the earlier afternoon by the lake. She'd felt free then; the hospital setting had drained her spirit.

The movie ended and Marsh rose to go.

"Feeling any better?" he asked Randi.

"Yeah."

"Great. Sleep tight, Baby. I'll drop by and check on you tomorrow." He bent over and kissed her goodnight. Stopping by Erin's chair on the way out the door, he bent over and brushed her cheek lightly. "Goodnight."

She stood up.

"Do you want me to see about getting you a cot in here?"

"I don't know. They have extras this time of night?"

"You need one. I should have asked earlier. It won't hurt to ask. I'll see about it on the way out."

He paused a moment longer, slid his arms around her, pressed her to him, kissed her lips gently. He stood looking into her eyes for a full minute. Then he was gone.

Erin walked to the doorway and stood looking out into the already semi-darkened corridor. Doors on the opposite side of the hallway were almost all closed to provide sufficient motivation for patients to sleep. She watched Marsh at the nurse's station for a few minutes, then get on the elevator. Nurses bustled from one side of the hall to the other to answer lights above still-opened doors. Trays of this and that. An extra pillow and blanket here and there. The head nurse was busily writing at the nurse's desk. Hospitals presented a most depressing sight at this time of night. The shadow fostered melancholy with or without illness. Erin was glad she'd come back to spend the night with Randi, if for no other reason than to dispel her own depression.

Was she right in insisting to Marsh that they tell Randi? The doctor hadn't supported either of them during their first conference but had volunteered to tell her for them if they wanted him to. Yet he had not seemed unhappy with their decision to wait a while. But when you tell her, he'd said, don't take away her hope. What parent could take away hope when that's all they had to offer?

Did the doctor really expect a cure? An unrelenting remission? Something about his eyes suggested that he did. Erin hung on to that look, recalled it repeatedly as a basis for her own hope.

Marsh had long since disappeared into the elevator at the far end of the hallway. Erin turned back into the room, got her make-up bag, and went into the bathroom. After removing her make-up, she puttered around a few minutes longer, then settled down into the large upholstered chair.

"That's not going to be too comfortable to sleep in," Randi said as her mother took a seat and spread the extra blanket over her arms and legs. "How long you think before they'll bring a bed?"

"No telling. This'll be okay. I can sleep in anything," she lied.

"It really wasn't necessary for you to come back. I already feel better."

"Good. You look better. But I came back because I wanted to. . . . Hospitals can be lonesome."

"You're telling me. Creepy. This afternoon before you and Daddy got here, it was like . . . I don't know. I felt . . . far away from everybody."

Both mother and daughter sat quietly for a few minutes.

"What did Mike say?"

"He said okay. He was surprised you were still in the hospital."

"I thought he'd know. I wasn't at school."

"He said to tell you he wanted to come see you anyway."

There was another silence. Erin got up and turned on the TV news. At 10:20 she switched the set off again and sat back down to get comfortable for the night. The nurse brought in an extra blanket, which she wrapped snuggly around her feet. She pushed the chair, mummy style, back into the corner and propped the pillow next to the wall.

"Mother, why aren't I getting any better?"

"It . . . just takes time for these kinds of things to get under control. . . . Your system has to absorb the drug."

Silence.

Erin felt as though she'd answered the darkness. She could not remember ever having lied to her daughter. She even hated evading her questions as she had just done—so few she ever asked her.

She had a right to know. She was not the type who'd want to be protected. Protected? Erin could imagine how her eyes would flash with rage, resentment when she found out she'd been lied to. Then they'd soften with embarrassment and shame that they'd not trusted her with the truth. Her very own truth. Marsh was protecting himself, not Randi. If she asked outright, . . . she'd tell her. Whether Marsh agreed or not.

Randi turned over and went to sleep.

Thirteen

When Marsh walked into the hospital room, he knew the elderly patient hovered near death. Being around the hospital routinely, he could sense approaching death in a patient's countenance. Cancer had ravished her body; there was nothing to be done but to increase her pain medication from day to day.

Doctors and nurses, unable to handle their own fears of death and failure to cure, avoided her now. Nevertheless, the patient needed someone's presence and had asked that the chaplain be called. The woman's only son, who lived out of state, had come to stay days at a time when the doctor or nurse had phoned to say that this was "the day." Still she lingered. Her son had not been able to come this time; she was dying alone.

Marsh approached the small, fragile body lying beneath the smooth sheets, unrumpled despite the night's use. The patient faced the window. He walked around to the other side of the bed, took her hand from its resting place on the bedrail, and held it to his breast.

"Thank you . . . coming," she whispered.

Marsh bent closer to her face. "What can I do to make you more comfortable?"

"Stay, please." She closed her eyes again.

He drug the chair from the foot of the bed around to the side so she could see him, should she open her eyes again. He usually prayed with patients, especially with Mrs. Wibble, on regular visits. However, this morning she was not conscious enough to ask him to do so. He closed his eyes, but his thoughts defied coherent expression. He breathed deeply, consciously tried to draw in more air. Pray. He should pray.

He gazed around the room. Cracks of early morning sunlight came in along the sides of the drapes. No extra gowns or robes hung from the hook on the back of the door. No clutter. Even the water pitcher sat in the exact spot where the nurse's aide placed it every day. No flowers. One artificial ivy, no doubt from her son, sat on the floor in the corner. No books, no writing paper, pens. Completely barren. She had already been removed from life.

His short sleeve shirt left his bare arms cold; he shivered. Where was God? All those years of reading, studying. Were they empty theories? "Just reach out, God is there," he'd told people. Emptiness now. He could not will himself to pray. He fixed his eyes on the tiny child-size figure before him. She lay so still, her eyes closed, breathing noiselessly. He recalled hearing the loud wheezing from Matt's bedroom so many nights. The coughing. The gasping for air. Matt's crying that he couldn't breathe. Getting up and running into his brother's bedroom. Cowering helplessly in the corner of the room while his parents tried to prop his brother up, comfort him, decide whether to take him to the hospital. The big oxygen tent stretched over his hospital bed. The harried look on his parents' faces. He had sat between them at Matt's bedside, tried to hold his mother's hand, make her feel better. He'd assured them that he was praying for the wheezing and coughing to be stopped by morning. His parents had always smiled condescendingly and directed their attention back to Matt.

Mrs. Wibble stirred slightly. He stood up and walked to her side again, patted her hand. His own daughter lay in a hospital bed across town; he held a woman's hand he hardly knew.

He patted, waited.

The elderly woman's breathing grew fainter. Marsh leaned closer to her. The breathing stopped. He stood staring at her for a full minute, then bent over and kissed her forehead. He stepped to the doorway, summoned the nurse, then turned and walked down the hall without waiting.

* * *

The coffee shop was crowded; Marsh took a seat anyway. Except when called to the hospital early, he rarely stopped in for breakfast. Two off-duty nurses in the booth behind him discussed the night's emergencies over donuts and coffee. Various other hospital personnel loitered in the vicinity prior to beginning their respective duties. The whole area seemed cramped, stifling. The completion of the new wing had cleared the halls of carpenters and ladders only to replace them with more patients and nurses. Always crowds, even around death.

He pulled out his billfold, looked through it, and stuck it back in his pocket. Mrs. Wibble had scribbled her son's phone number on a slip of paper and given it to him a few days ago. She'd already given him the number twice before and he'd filed it in his office. He'd wait an hour or two before calling. Let the doctor notify the son and family first.

Marsh ordered eggs and toast and then leaned back to drink his coffee, realizing he wasn't hungry enough to eat anything. It was too early to call Randi.

"Hello, Marsh."

The chaplain looked up to see Sandy, holding a napkin-enveloped sweetroll, standing beside his table.

"Have a seat," he offered.

"No, can't. Just got off and stopped by here to

grab a few more calories before going home to sleep."

Marsh didn't feel up to chatter, but he asked, "How are things going? Losing any more cars?"

"No." She slid into the opposite side of the booth. "No. it may be a while before I get another one to lose."

"Having trouble with the insurance?"

"Well, standard policy I think for stolen cars. They're going to wait thirty days to see if the police locate it before they'll pay off."

"So what are you doing for transportation in the meantime? They pay for a rent-a-car?"

"Are you kidding? They offer fifteen a day. That wouldn't rent the backseat."

"I bet you're right."

"So I'm sponging off my friends in the meantime." Her eyes lit up with a mischievous grin making her look even more girlish than her petite size.

"By the way, are you a friend?"

"Well, that depends—you need a ride?"

"As a matter of fact I do. Otherwise I'm going to have to hang around an hour until Jody gets off." She paused, grinned coyly. Then, "Well, friend or foe?"

"Let me think on it awhile."

The waitress came with his eggs. He pushed them from one side of the plate to the other not bothering to salt or pepper them.

"Listen," she began again, "I owe you an apology."

"What?"

"For walking out, I mean."

"Accepted," Marsh shrugged. "Counselors get used to that sort of thing."

She gazed at him intently for a moment. "That's why I owe you an apology. You're not just my counselor. Are you?" She reached out and ran her forefinger over the back of his hand.

He looked back to the eggs.

"I really care what you think, Marsh. I guess that's why I walked out. It hurt my pride when you didn't side with me." She withdrew her hand, picked up his water glass and took a long sip, eyeing him over the rim.

She set the glass down. "Let's just say it wasn't one of my better days and forget it."

"Sure."

They sat for a few moments, the rattle of Marsh's spoon as he stirred his coffee the only noise between them.

"Things aren't any better between you and Steve?"

"Not really. Oh, maybe. I don't know. I guess I'm just too bored right now to take our marital temperature. We're not arguing as much if that's what you mean."

"That's not the thermometer, exactly."

"He's so absorbed in the hospital that he can't see I exist right now."

"You're part of that world, aren't you? You know his patients, his cases?"

"Sure, some of them. But I don't eat and sleep

them. He can't turn it off when he comes home like I can." She toyed with the sweetroll a moment. "I bet you don't take all this home with you, do you?"

"Not often. I guess not."

"I really admire that in a man. The ability to be top in his field and make a woman happy, too."

He looked down again, stirred his coffee.

"You are married, aren't you?"

"Yes."

Silence.

"Maybe when Steve gets a little more established—like you—confident of himself, he can relax a little. Give me something."

Marsh knew where she was leading, could read her eyes. "Established," she'd called him. He studied her face. A pert nose, little make-up, blonde hair swinging chin length. The excitement in her voice, as if something earth-shaking might happen any minute. Take her home? God knows he needed someone to talk to now. Lean on. Someone who took care of dying patients every day, who really knew what death was. Take her home?

Erin's face surged into his consciousness. Hers and Sandy's personality differences were so much more than the ten years between them indicated. Erin was beautiful, would always be beautiful even at sixty. Her eyes demanded attention. Erin spoke, loved, motivated with her eyes. Her image possessed him against his will.

Sandy was chattering on about something Steve had said the night before about one particular patient and how she couldn't believe he could get so involved in such a minor case.

"Marsh, how long do I give him?" The lightness, nonchalance of a moment earlier, gone. "How long do I give him to make it on the job and come back to me?"

"As long as you can."

She looked away, toyed with the corner of the napkin holding her roll. Marsh sat sipping his coffee. He knew he was not saying what she wanted, expected to hear. He needed her invitation, her admiration. He thought of other clients, other conversations. But he'd never stepped over the line. Sandy knew that now.

They sat quietly for a few minutes more, listening to the morning chatter around them. Maintenance people, delivery men in and out.

"Listen, if you're not going to give me that ride, I'd better be sure to catch Jody."

She picked up the sweetroll and rose to go. Marsh stood with her. Their eyes met, then she was gone.

Before she was out of the coffee shop, someone at the last table called to her. She stopped, said something low and laughed heartily. Her voice trailed behind to those seated at nearby tables. This was one of those moments when Marsh longed for the freedom to unleash his thoughts on someone who'd let him be a man rather than a chaplain.

He thought of Steve, his hesitancy to admit their marital problems. He'd be angry if he knew Sandy had been confiding in him. He asked for a third cup of coffee and reflected on other couples he'd counseled.

Joseph and Karla Kendricks. Karla had been the one to dump their problems in his lap. Joseph faced a malpractice suit in which the plantiff claimed he'd operated while under the influence of alcohol. Marsh had stepped in at that point of their deteriorating situation and worked with them for over three years. Although Joseph was acquitted, Marsh finally led him to acknowledge his alcoholism and to put his life back in order. Other such couples, as well as individual clients, fluttered through Marsh's consciousness. He'd felt a confident and capable counselor before; he would again. Just hold on a little tighter, Marsh coaxed himself. A little tighter.

It was 7:30. Certainly Randi would be awake and ready to answer the phone. He walked back to his office to call. His first appointment wasn't until 9:30; he decided to drive over instead.

Before getting to the car, he stopped. The blood donors. He hadn't done anything about getting donors. Well, that could wait. He resumed his pace. He knew hospitals; they wouldn't deny the transfusions for lack of immediate donors. It could at least wait until after he saw Randi. Maybe Erin could take care of that. She probably already had. He got in the car and drove off.

"How's my girl?" he asked when Randi responded to his knock. He noted the color change in her complexion since the night before. His spirits lifted.

Erin stepped out of the bathroom dressed for work.

"Has the doctor been around this morning?"

"No, not yet."

"Do you think he'll let her come home today?"

"I wouldn't think so. He'll have to keep her long enough to see how this new drug does."

"We can do that at home, can't we, Randi?" He turned back to his daughter.

"I guess so."

"What's this 'I guess' business?"

She didn't answer. Erin looked at her husband with such intensity that he could feel her gaze.

"I'm going on to work. I'll call you later," Erin said to Randi.

"Okay."

She expected her daughter to say more but then mentally scolded herself for the expectation. How could she ever reach her? Get on the same emotional plane? It couldn't all be Marsh's fault; she'd been with her all night without making contact. One night couldn't make up for a lifetime; she was expecting too much. She picked up her purse and walked on out into the hall.

Marsh closed the door behind her, pulled up a chair beside the bed and sat down. Unable to see Randi's face clearly, he stood up again.

"Now, tell me again. How do you really feel this morning?"

"Better."

"You look good."

Marsh brushed her side bangs back from her forehead, then quickly pulled his hand away remembering how that gesture of childhood had come to annoy her in the past couple of years.

"I feel pretty good, except for my hair. Would you plug in the hot rollers for me? I want to get my hair done before they do whatever they're going to do to me today. So I'll be ready when Mike comes."

"Is he coming by?" Marsh walked over and plugged in the hot curlers. "I thought you told your mother to tell him not to come?"

"I did. But I changed my mind. He'll come anyway. Either on his lunch hour or after school."

"I thought you two were having a little trouble."

"We were. But I quit harping about his pickup truck."

"Like it now?"

"Are you kidding? I decided it was a lost cause. That thing'll be with him to the grave."

Marsh flinched, turned back to the curlers. "Look at it like this—you're always in style at rodeos."

"Big deal. I'd just as soon leave those off, too."

"Well, you are down on your kicker friends, aren't you?"

Randi turned over on her side. A panicked expression spread over her face. She shivered and tilted her head, chin high.

"I'm sick to my stomach. Get me a washcloth."

Marsh dashed around the bed to the bathroom, wet a cloth and placed it on her forehead. Randi's face was ashen, her breathing slow and soft. The picture of Mrs. Wibble forged into his consciousness. His stomach knotted up; he squeezed his daughter's hand tighter.

She darted for the bathroom. Some of the color had returned to her face when she crawled back into bed a few minutes later.

"Daddy, why aren't I getting any better?"

"You are." He swallowed hard. "You are."

"I don't feel like it. They keep switching me from one thing to another and keep taking blood and giving blood."

"I explained all about that when they first put you in."

"Yeah, I know." Randi averted her eyes and grew quiet.

Marsh leaned against the foot of the bed and surveyed the room. Rumpled sheets, her robe draped over the back of the chair, notebook paper scattered on the top of the bureau. Much like her bedroom at home. Full of activity, life. It reassured him.

"Do you think Michael will be by at lunch? if he's coming, I won't bother you then."

"I don't know. Maybe."

"Is he riding this weekend?"

"No. He's not entering yet, just practicing."

"Well, if he's practicing, it won't take long until the fever strikes good."

"Why did Mother spend the night here last night?" Randi lifted her eyes to his again.

"She just wanted to, I guess. What'd she tell you?"

"The same thing. . . . But she's acting different, you know? She's starting to . . . hover over me, . . . just since I've been sick lately."

"She's a little too late with that, isn't she?" Marsh regretted the remark immediately.

Randi turned back to face him. She stared at him for a long time without saying anything. Then, "Daddy, would you tell me the truth if I asked you something?"

"Sure. Ask it, and I'll run it through the computer here." He pointed to his temple. "See if I can get a total printout."

"Daddy, please. I'm serious. . . . I want to know if you'll honestly tell me the truth?"

Something in Marsh twisted, pulling tightly the muscles around the chest cavity and stomach. He couldn't keep up the merry-ho-ho routine, but all within him fought succumbing to her seriousness.

"Okay," he said finally.

"I'm not getting any better. And please don't say I am. I'm tired all the time. This is just like it was when I came in here the first time."

Marsh waited, squeezing her hand softly until she got to the point.

"Would you tell me—if it was something else I had? Would you tell me if it wasn't anemia?" Her voice was soft, but under control. No tears.

"Sure I would, Baby. Of course, I would." Marsh leaned over to embrace her, pulling her up to him. "Everything's all right. You're going to be all right and out of here in no time." He held her against his shoulder so she could not see his face.

When he was in control again, he released her. She lay back on the bed, a faraway look in her eyes. That was the first time he'd ever lied to her, and somehow he felt she could sense the deception even through their embrace. He could not bring himself to reassure her again.

He walked around to the other side of the room and sat down. Randi replaced the cloth on her forehead.

"We haven't forgotten you." A nurse poked her head in the door. "We'll be in with clean linens in a few minutes."

Having glanced toward the door, Randi saw her hot rollers on the bureau. "Just turn those off," she gestured toward them. "I can't do it right now."

Marsh did as she asked. She was pale again.

"I think I'll go and let you try to get to sleep. Maybe you can sleep it off."

Randi never turned her head to look at her dad but held it rigidly toward the ceiling as if any movement might push her over the brink again.

Marsh patted her hand and left.

Fourteen

Erin felt drawn to Randi's room as an artist to an unfinished canvas. She longed to fill in the faint outline of their relationship. Yet the awesomeness of the project frightened her.

When she stopped by to see her at noon Friday, Randi's face was still swollen, especially her nose. Dark rings encircled her eyes. Erin decided that it was the light pink pajamas which made the dark circles more prominent.

"I hope I'm not cutting in on Mike's time?" Erin asked from the doorway.

"No, he's not here."

"I would have called first to check, but I thought I'd surprise you." Erin edged nearer the bed and looked at the almost untouched lunch tray. "Have you had any company?"

"Daddy."

"Oh."

"And Carrie and Meganne were by on their lunch period."

"What'd they have to say?"

"Nothing much."

Erin picked up the history book lying on the end of the bed. "Have you felt like doing any homework?"

"A little. I read one chapter. I'm really going to be behind."

"How much can you miss in two days?"

"A lot. They really start cramming everything in at the last quarter."

"Can't they keep a running list of your assignments for you? I could pick them up, and you could be doing some of it along as you feel like it?"

"I wouldn't feel like it much—even if I had them."

"Maybe the nausea won't last too much longer."

The greeting card lying on the bedside table caught Erin's eye. She picked it up and read: "Get well quick. Who do you think you are. . . ." Inside it said, "Skipping out on us?" A long-eared rabbit in a skirt and high-heels pouted from the page. Carrie had signed it, "Will you ever forgive me? Love, Carrie." Erin returned the card to the table.

"I guess Carrie feels pretty bad about the nosebleed."

"Uh huh."

Silence.

Erin picked up the history book again, thumbed through the chapter Randi had marked, and then laid it aside.

"Has Mike been by at all?" Erin asked.

"No."

Randi didn't explain; Erin didn't press for details. Ten minutes she'd been in her daughter's room. The question, the answer, the silence.

It was obvious that Randi hadn't been up and down the halls visiting with other patients. If she had, she'd have said at least something about what was going on—even if just to comment on the lack of appropriate company. Erin re-examined the lunch tray, took a bite of the jello.

Randi flipped the TV game show off.

"I've been here three days. What's really wrong with me?"

Erin drew in her breath slowly and stared into her daughter's face. Her eyes pleaded and dared at the same time. Marsh's words echoed in her mind, demanded. Yet Randi was asking her, not her daddy. She needed an honest answer to a legitimate question.

"What's wrong with me?" Randi repeated.

"You have leukemia, Randi."

Randi's face grew white; she lay back very still, staring up at the ceiling. Erin, not knowing whether to rush ahead with explanations of hope or to stop and give her time to take in the shock, waited.

Then, "I don't want you to be scared. The doctors know what they're doing, and this medicine and chemotherapy are going to get you in remission again. If it doesn't, they'll try something else. It's a matter of waiting to find the right drug—the one that'll work for you."

There was a long silence.

"Why wouldn't Daddy tell me when I asked before?" Randi's eyes were full of tears.

Erin turned her daughter's question over and over, forming, then rejecting various answers. "It's not easy to tell someone you love something like . . . this."

Randi said nothing more. She stared straight up at the ceiling. Leaning against the bedside, Erin wanted to reach out, hold her, comfort her. Yet something held her back. Randi had never been the kind to welcome such affection, not since she was a small child. Erin could almost feel the tiny arms of a five-year-old push away, struggle for freedom. Erin stood with the pained expression of a mother watching her first grader on stage trying to remember her lines in the school play.

"Does Mike know? Is that why he hasn't been to see me?" Randi asked in a soft, child-like tone.

"Mike doesn't know. Nobody knows but your dad and I." Erin reached out and patted Randi's arm, rubbing it back and forth, unconsciously kneading the muscle and slight fold of skin.

"Please don't tell anybody."

"Of course not, if that's what you want."

"They'll be afraid of me."

"Who?"

"The kids at school. They'll treat me funny. Weird. Like they do Bojo." Randi referred to a senior who was confined to a wheelchair. Erin recalled seeing kids wheel him into the gym before basketball games.

"That's so different, Hon."

"No, it's not."

"Everybody likes Bojo anyway; I've heard you say it. He goes to the ballgames."

"Yeah. They like him, but that's not what I mean. He's just different. He doesn't get invited places. . . . Don't you understand?"

Erin nodded that she did. Then, "But with you, it's different. You're strong and just as good-looking as ever."

Randi turned away. Tears started to roll down her cheeks.

"Will my hair come out?"

"I . . . don't know, Randi. Maybe not. Everybody reacts differently to the chemotheraphy. Maybe it won't affect you that way at all."

Randi lay back on the pillow again, stared up at the ceiling.

"But how did I get it?"

Erin's facial expression never changed; she felt a rising lump in her throat. Drawing in her breath, she held it momentarily before exhaling short unsteady spurts.

"There's no way to tell exactly. . . . The doctors don't know what causes it. . . . Maybe a virus, they think." Erin drew in another deep breath trying to keep her voice even by talking through the short gasps for air. "And some researchers think it . . . might be caused from the atmosphere. From things like radiation in the air."

"What radiation?"

"From the nuclear testing sites, for one thing."

"They're not doing that here."

"They used to. When you were little. Before you can remember."

"Is that what did it?" Randi's voice was inquisitive, like a young child asking why leopards have spots.

"I don't know," Erin answered. "I think there's going to be a story in the newspaper in a few days about that."

"I just can't believe it, you know. I just can't believe it."

Erin reached over the invisible wall between them. Randi accepted her embrace and quietly sobbed in her mother's arms.

When Erin got back to the office, things were going at their usual hectic mid-afternoon pace. Research clerks bustled in and out of the file section, elbowed around each other from drawer to drawer.

She had driven slowly on the return trip, not

sure her emotions would be under control by the time she reached the office. Yet, sure they must be. Nothing about her conduct would betray Randi's plea that no one know.

Ralph waved from the back part of the hallway. "Remember me?"

"Now, let me see. Should I?"

"You know, the one that dropped that typed report, the twenty-one page, magnificently organized and worded report on your 'in' box at approximately 9:09 Tuesday morning?"

"Oh, that Ralph," Erin's words sounded light; her eyes betrayed.

"I'm sorry. I'll get to them as soon as I can."

He smiled and came toward her. "By the way, how's you daughter?"

"Fine, thank you." Erin went into her office.

He batted the door open after her before she could take a seat behind the desk.

"Then you can come to the party tonight at Freda's?"

"What did you say?" Freda shot up out of her chair.

Ralph turned around. "I asked Erin if she was coming to the party at your place." Then back to Erin, "Did you get one of these?" He waved a memo in her direction.

"Let me see that." Freda took it out of his hand and read.

"Yeah, I think this is really a nice idea having the entire department over. I mean we hardly ever get together. Christmas, that's about all."

Freda stood gaping at the memo, which was an invitation to the entire research department and their "dates or spouses" to come to a "little get-together" at her place.

"What are we going to do? You've got everything worked out, I guess. I bet you really know how to throw a party, Freda."

"Where did you get this?" She stood re-reading the memo.

"Off my desk. Just a while ago. But don't worry. Word'll get around all right, I saw June and Mack's invitation earlier this morning. Everybody I talked to is coming; don't worry. Word'll get around." He put his arm around her shoulder patronizingly. "They'll come, they'll come."

"Who did this?"

"Did what?"

"Who put this out?"

"You're asking me who sent out invitations to your party?"

"Did you do this? This is your idea of a joke? Do you know what I have planned for tonight?"

"No, but don't tell me. Let it be a surprise. I love surprises."

"Ralph, who did this? Did everybody get one of these?"

"I said don't worry. If they didn't, they'll get the word from somebody who did."

"I'm going to have to go around to everybody in this entire office and tell them. . . ."

"They'll come, they'll come."

"You did this. I know it had to be you."

Ralph ushered her back out of Erin's office, winked over his shoulder, and closed the door behind them.

Erin shook her head and shooed him out. She sat down and tried to tune out the voices which continued outside the door. Another one of Ralph's "boredom-battlers," as he called them. She finished going through the correspondence left from the morning's mail and found two letters which needed immediate attention. The voices had stopped; she buzzed Freda.

"Bring in the file on the Hile project and see if that letter from David Carson is in there."

Freda pulled the Hile report from the files almost immediately, but the letter was not included. She searched through the miscellaneous correspondence, the file for recent grant requests, the file for grants-under-consideration, and turned up no letter.

"Here's the report," she said handing the project folder to Erin. "But I haven't gotten my hands on the letter yet. And by the way. About the party. That was Ralph's idea of a joke."

"So I gathered."

Freda smirked.

Erin took the report and thumbed through it thinking her secretary might have possibly missed the letter.

"By the way, how's Randi today?"

"Better, thank you."

"I went by to give blood. Several others said they did too."

"I really appreciate it. When I checked with the donor receptionist, she said we had fifteen to donate—three extras."

"That's great." The secretary nodded her head vigorously. "That's just great. Aren't people good when you need them? I mean, it's nice to have friends to count on. And it does people good to feel needed, useful, don't you think? To feel like they're really doing something important for somebody." Freda stopped nodding. "I bet your daughter is dying to get back to school, though."

The word flashed like a neon light. Erin continued to listen politely to the prattle. Freda talked so slowly, phrased and rephrased each thought. Erin wanted to help her pull the words out. But at least her voice filled the hours so that she didn't have to concentrate on work.

"Yeah, missing a lot of school is tough on a kid nowadays. Always was," Freda continued.

"Randi usually manages to stay caught up."

"She must be a pretty good student."

"She is."

"That's important now. Grades. Of course, good grades makes it easier on them in college."

Erin did not permit herself to think beyond

getting Randi adjusted from one drug to the next. She felt like a long-distance swimmer trying to find a comfortable pace.

Freda continued, completely oblivious to the errand which had brought her into her boss' office. "I guess she's probably already made her mind up about where she's going to college. The school counselors really push them to do that, don't they? They always did push mine. Had them in there discussing where to send SAT and ACT scores before my kids ever thought about taking the tests."

By the time Freda finished her monologue, Erin had forgotten the questions which preceded it. She stared blankly at Freda's large floral print dress.

"I'll get the letter to you as soon as I can," Freda said, suddenly sensitive to Erin's inattention.

What letter was it she wanted? A glance at the project before her brought the whole matter back. She had wanted the copy of the letter from David Carson about the extension of his due date on the work he was doing. The sponsors of the project were impatient for the finished findings, and she needed to get in touch with them about the postponement.

To the second letter. Somehow, Bleyl and Bleyl had received the initial report including procedures and the questionnaire used on the textile employees' survey but had never received the compilation of all the answers, the summary statements and recommendations. At least she could take care of that easily enough. Their mistake had already been caught, and the already typed, correct and complete document lay on her desk ready for final approval and mailing.

She called Freda in again, dictated the letter of apology about the oversight, and asked her to see that it was sent out immediately by one of the girls up front.

Now what? All she could think about was Randi alone in her hospital room across town. The silent tears. The anguish in her expression. She'd tried to stay longer at noon, but Randi had acted as if she wanted to be alone. Maybe she should call. But what else could she say?

She sat dazed, staring at the pages in front of her without seeing them. What would Marsh say when he found out she'd told her? No, she'd done the right thing; Randi wanted to know, needed to know. Just this once, Randi had needed her—to tell her the truth.

And this time she was there.

"I found it." Freda stuck her head around the door, then walked on in and handed the missing letter to her supervisor. Erin took the copy and read while Freda waited.

"That's just as I remembered. Write a letter to Hile and tell them that Carson will have his work in to us at the end of this month. Attach a copy of this letter to it."

"Okay, sure. I'm glad I retrieved that one."

Freda heaved a sigh. "Thought I never would see it again."

Before she was completely out the door, she swung the floral print to a pause and added, "I guess you're glad to have this off your mind, aren't you?

Erin's smile was frozen.

Fifteen

The editor of the *Daily Mirror* looked up when his reporter, Leon Howard, walked into the office.

"Got something for you. Right down your alley," the editor said.

"What?"

"The radiation thing. An official from Bending and Dowden called a couple days ago. Been waiting for you to get back in town."

"Yeah?"

The editor reared back in his chair, hands behind his head. His collar gapped open in newsman fashion. "Seems somebody turned up an unpublished study done ten years ago. Shows a definite link between radiation from nuclear testing sites and leukemia."

"I knew it. I knew it," Howard wagged his head and wiped the oily shine from his chin. "When are we going to get a look at it?"

"You're supposed to meet her at the Holiday Inn Coffee Shop Monday morning at ten."

"Her?"

"She didn't identify herself."

The reported headed for the door. "Be right back." He returned a few minutes later with a file and spread its contents on the corner of the already cluttered desk while the editor shuffled papers and pretended to create an empty place.

"Hit me with a few angles," the editor gestured toward the file's contents. "What you got there?"

"Plenty. I've been waiting for this." Howard lifted a newspaper clipping from the pile, studied it, then tossed it aside. "That's on the 1953 Upshot-Knothole series. And this. Six tons of roetgens of activity on St George, Utah. . . . 'Stay indoors' they said."

He pulled a third paper to the top of the file. "The fusion weapons, the hydrogen bombs, are more powerful than the fission ones, the atom bombs," he explained. "That's why all this gobbledygook in the press releases. Thermonuclear, fusion, hydrogen—a few hot words like those just happen to be missing."

Logan leaned backward again in his chair and nodded. Howard continued shuffling through the file's contents. He examined papers, clippings, charts, one after the other, then replaced them in careful fashion, as if each were a highly classified treasure rather than a readily accessible press release.

"They sent out one radio announcement.

Advised people to stay indoors from nine to noon as a *precautionary* measure." Howard smirked. "If you don't listen to the radio, you're out of luck."

"What else?"

"I've got copies of the studies the AEC kept quoting." The reporter flipped through the title pages and moved them to the bottom of the stack. "The 'threshold hypothesis.' Safe dosages. They keep forgetting it's a theory, not fact."

"What's that?" Logan pointed to a couple of photostatted half-sheets.

"Got a couple of memos between two senators debating whether we ought to pay for damages if somebody sues. Gerard. Winley. They're considering some sort of blanket payment to victims."

"Any figures discussed?"

"No, why?"

"I just wondered how much a senator figured it was worth to die of thyroid cancer." The reporter glanced up at his boss, then down again.

"What else?"

"Here's some figures on livestock deaths. Nevada. Utah. Arizona."

"Have you got anything on any specific lawsuits filed?"

"I don't remember. I'll have to look back through the other files."

"How about the number of cancer cases reported?"

"Yeah, I've got the figures somewhere. Over five hundred, if I remember correctly."

"Do you know if Bending and Dowden has been in on any of this earlier research?"

"Not for a fact. If they've got part of the contract, chances are they were in it from the first."

"There you go again—jumping to logical conclusions. This is the government, remember?"

Howard shrugged. "We'll see when I get the chance to question . . . whoever . . . Monday."

"You think she'll really know anything?"

"How should I know? You talked to her."

"May be some peon wanting to feel important. It's about my turn for another one of those."

"Pretty high stakes, wouldn't you say?"

Logan wrinkled his forehead inquisitively.

"If it costs her job."

"You planning to guarantee her anonymity?"

"Promise her anything," Howard sang the lyrics.

The editor shook his head and waved him out. Howard gathered up the file's contents and headed toward the door. "I'm going to finish up the Newman story, then get right on this."

"Hope this isn't going to be a wild goose chase—you get stood up Monday," Logan added before Howard was out of earshot.

"Why? She sound edgy to you?"

"They always do."

The reporter jerked his head to the side in a shrug and disappeared around the corner.

Erin walked through the den where Marsh was sitting, straight back to the bedroom to get out of her high heels. After having been gone overnight, she noted the stale air and raised a bedroom window. She'd been by the clinic after work to pick up her overnight bag and had offered to stay the night again. But Randi had insisted she'd rather be alone, mentioning that she didn't want to be "any trouble." Erin couldn't help read Marsh into that statement.

She passed back by Randi's bedroom door. The darkened room screamed at her. The poster-making materials which she'd gathered up after the quick trip to the emergency room lay untouched. Randi's school clothes from that afternoon still hung on the closet door. All the signs of life, but no Randi. She turned and walked on back to the den.

Marsh looked up from the paper. She edged around his feet, not meeting his eyes. Dinner, always her responsibility. She leaned against the kitchen cabinet. So tired. It was an effort to lift her arms. Her neck and shoulders ached. The night's sleep in the chair hadn't helped.

"Do you want to drive in to Jackson and get a bite to eat?" she called to Marsh from the kitchen.

"Why didn't you bring some hamburgers or something?"

"I didn't think about it."

Silence. She waited.

"Do you?" she asked again after a moment.

"I'm not really hungry."

"Neither am I, but I'm so . . . tired."

"Come here, then."

She walked around the corner and stood. He reached out his hand for hers and slipped out of the chair onto the floor. She took his hand and let him pull her down on top of him. He lifted her arms and stretched them way above his head. Pressing her breasts full against his chest, he rocked her gently back and forth. She relaxed, stretched out full length on him. He stopped the rocking motion and massaged her neck and shoulders slowly, thoroughly. She moaned, breathed deep and full.

"That feels so good. I'll give you a couple of hours to stop."

"Did they ever get around to bringing a cot last night?"

"This morning. About 3:30 when the new shift came on."

"Well, I told 'em. I'm sorry."

"It's okay." Then, "Marsh, I need to get out, away for a while. Just get a salad, pizza, something quick."

Silence.

"Are you going to the hospital tonight?" she asked after a moment.

"No. I spent most of the morning over there. I phoned her about middle of the afternoon. She didn't have much to say except that she didn't want me to come by again."

Erin said nothing.

"She and Mike must be having trouble. . . . But she usually mentions something like that."

"Had Mike been there when you phoned?" Erin asked.

"No. Why?"

"Randi's been expecting him all day. He never came by at lunch."

"Hmmm."

There was another long silence. She should tell him about telling Randi. But he'd be angry. His hands felt so good on her. He'd worked her dress up around her waist, was rubbing her hips, the small of her back. Kneading her flesh, pressing her to him. He slid one hand up her side to her chin, pulled her face up to his lips and kissed her mouth, then eyelids. Then he pressed her head into his neck. She kissed him over and over on the neck.

They lay quietly together for a few mintues, she still stretched out on top of him, feeling his chest expand and contract with each breath.

"You never answered. Do you want to go out to eat?" she asked finally.

Silence.

"I don't think so."

She held her head up to look him in the face.

"I just don't feel like going out when Randi's in the hospital."

"I don't mean somewhere special. I don't feel

like a celebration either. Just out. Somewhere quiet. To relax a while, think of something besides computers and hospitals."

"What would you tell Randi?"

"What do you mean what would I tell Randi? I'd tell her we went out to eat dinner."

Silence. He removed his hand from her breast, dropped both arms to the floor. Erin pushed herself up off him, sat beside him on the floor.

"Marsh, . . . staying home won't make her get well any faster. . . . We can't just . . . quit living. Be afraid to even laugh again. Make love, enjoy ourselves." Her eyes clouded; she lifted his hand, laid it in her lap.

He looked at her with a blank, uncomprehending stare. "I just can't." He turned his head away, stared out into space.

"What are you thinking about?" Her voice was hardly above a whisper.

"About one weekend when I asked Mom if I could go on a campout. A friend David and his dad invited me along. She started crying, Mom did. . . . Asking me how I could be so thoughtless. Wanting to go out and have fun while Matt was so sick. He'd been really sick. In the hospital. But he was better. . . . And she kept telling me how thoughtless I was and how I must not love my brother." He paused, continued to look away. "And he got really bad again that night and Mom called Dad and me at home and told us to come to the hospital as quick as we could. I kept thinking what if . . . what if I'd been gone with David. Out on the Gulf somewhere. And Matt had . . . died."

Erin sat looking at him for a long time, then slowly eased herself up and went back into the kitchen. She stood leaning against the refrigerator. Back where she was a half an hour ago. She still hadn't told him. Why? She had to. Before he went to see her again.

Abruptly, she took out cheese for grilled cheese sandwiches. No, a salad. She should use up the raw vegetables, which had been in the refrigerator for over a week. She pulled the lettuce, celery, cucumbers from the bottom drawer. Still with her back to Marsh, who'd come in to sit at the kitchen table, she began to chop. The celery squirmed; strings entwined her wet fingers.

She could hear the newspaper rustle as he turned the pages. She stopped and faced him.

"Marsh, . . ." He looked up. "I told her this afternoon."

"You . . ."

"She asked me."

"We agreed . . ."

"I just couldn't lie to her. She knew. She's suspected it ever since she went back in Wednesday. Since the nosebleed. You know she asked you yesterday what was wrong, and you wouldn't tell her."

Marsh stalked out of the house slamming the door behind him. Erin listened as he pulled out of the driveway and sped off. The gravel crunched, echoed his anger. Why couldn't he see that keeping a blanket over Randi's head wouldn't help? That everybody didn't deal with problems like he did?

It was almost as if improving one relationship meant losing the other. She recalled his words about Matt; anger gave way to pity. Why couldn't they help rather than hurt each other? Her eyes filled again. What would he do after she talked to the reporter on Monday?

Sixteen

Marsh spent Friday night at Memorial, too angry to go back home to Erin, too afraid to see Randi.

He dropped by her room Saturday afternoon. "Can I come in?" he asked, sticking his head around the door.

"Uh, huh."

Randi sat in the chair by the window, back to the door, her feet propped on the window ledge.

"How you feeling? No, wait. . . ." Marsh raised his hands in protest. "Now think about it; I want a good report." He smiled broadly, his eyebrows raised in a clownish expression.

"Fine." Randi looked back to her magazine.

"Fine? Is that all the details I get?"

Randi looked up again and studied her dad's face in a strained manner.

"No more nausea? No more sore nose?"

"Not much."

"Great. That's great." Marsh exaggerated his

nod, stood with hands in his pockets, jangled his keys. Then sauntering around the room, he picked up *Seventeen*, then a grammar book, a literature book, examining each in studious detail.

"Who brought all these?"

"Meganne. Carrie."

"Mike been by?"

"No. He called."

"Is he coming up tonight to see you?"

"He didn't say."

"Say, what's with these long answers?" Marsh sat down on the ledge beside Randi's feet. She moved them and tucked them under her robe.

"I don't feel like talking."

"Something wrong between you and Mike?"

"I don't know."

Marsh felt relieved. A boyfriend problem.

"When did all this happen?"

"Now. . . . Last month. . . . Who knows?" Randi looked away.

"Picture's still not clear."

"I can't explain it any better." Her tone was short. She retucked the robe around her feet. "Things are just different, that's all. . . . He doesn't have anything to say when he calls. . . . He didn't come by yesterday."

"You told your mother to tell him you didn't want to see him."

"That was only one day. And because I didn't feel good."

"Maybe he's been busy."

"Maybe."

Silence.

"All he cares about are those horses. . . . And he spends more time talking to Carrie than he does me."

"Carrie? I thought she was your best friend?"

"She is." Randi answered softly and stared out the window overlooking the parking lot. She watched a driver pull forward, then back-up several times before maneuvering into a parking space.

Marsh studied her expression. How hurt was she? She wasn't crying, but then she seldom cried. The pupils in her eyes were dilated. From the drugs or the sunlight, Marsh couldn't decide. He'd not noticed until now how much her feelings were revealed in the expression around her eyes. She was like Erin in that regard—unable to hide her feelings. Even if she wouldn't admit them.

Marsh's face reddened. Mike—the thoughtless kid.

"I'm sorry you're hurt." Marsh leaned away from the window ledge and pecked her cheek. She didn't respond, still did not take her eyes from the scene outside the window.

Marsh got up and walked back to the foot of the bed where he picked up the Saturday paper, obviously untouched by Randi, and flipped through it.

"What's going on in the world?" he asked aloud.

She didn't answer. He read the front page.

"Well, then what else is going on here?"

"I'm ready to get outa here."

"If the medicine's not causing you any problems, you should be on your way."

She turned to look at him. "Then what? What happens after I go home? How much longer before I'm back?" Randi watched the back of her dad's neck. He did not turn to face her.

"I . . . I don't know that you'll ever have to come back. I hope not." His tone was flat, superficial.

She looked away. Her face locked into a fixed, nonexpressive mask. She sat facing the bright sunlight without blinking.

Despite the cool, late afternoon air, Mike wore cut-offs and a sleeveless shirt. He glanced toward the car pulling up to the curb in front of his house but continued to work on his truck.

Marsh sat in the car a moment looking straight ahead rather than toward the driveway. He felt uncomfortable in this neighborhood of split-level houses and odd-shaped lawns sloping up and down small hills. He'd had occasion to mention Randi's boyfriend's address to his acquaintances and did so with an aura of pride. However, viewing this streetful of affluent families now stirred anger rather than satisfaction. They were the men who'd known the right people at the right place at the right time. He'd suggested at one time that they investigate moving into this neighborhood, but he'd felt regret mixed with relief when Erin vetoed the idea. He hadn't even bothered to mention it again when she'd gotten the last promotion.

Roomy, comfortable, adequate suited her. She preferred to spend their extra money on nicer furniture, nicer accessories rather than a better address. He appreciated her knack for decorating, but the problem was that few of his friends had been inside his home. Address was all he had to show them; it was another form of definition. He gripped the steering wheel; he hated having others define him on circumstantial evidence.

He glanced in Mike's direction for the first time since pulling up to the curb. Men in these homes still fathered boys who proved to be rude, unfeeling, immature. Luck couldn't overcome that inadequacy. He slowly pushed open the car door and climbed out of the car. As if out for a leisurely late afternoon stroll, he glanced from side to side as he ambled up the driveway.

Mike stopped his drying maneuvers and stuck out his hand.

"Hi, Mr. Tilland."

"Hello, Michael."

Mike turned back to the truck, spread out the rag on the top of the cab, and pulled it slowly toward him in long, even strokes.

"Washing your truck, it'll probably rain."

"Probably. My luck."

Mike made a few last strokes across the cab and threw the rag to the side of the driveway. Marsh watched him. He felt awkward; he'd never talked to Randi's boyfriend except for perfunctory remarks. He was the first boy she had dated steadily.

"I came by to talk to you a few minutes . . . about you and Randi," Marsh said when Mike turned around to face him again.

"Yeah?"

"You and she are having a little trouble?"

"No, not that I know of." Reaching over to retrieve the cloth, Mike gave the side of the truck another swipe.

"Well, she seems to think so. . . . Not that she sent me over here. You don't mention this."

"Okay, I guess." Mike looked as though he had no idea what point Marsh was coming to.

"Do you still like her? Intend to date her anymore?"

"I feel kinda funny talking to you about this, Mr. Tilland. I . . ."

"Just answer what I asked you." Marsh's tone was harsher than he intended.

"Yes. Why?"

"You haven't been to see her?"

"I've been busy. Getting ready to ride in a rodeo."

Marsh nodded and paused a moment.

"You're not dating somebody else, too?"

"Well, maybe. . . . Look, I never told her she couldn't date anybody else. The same goes for me."

Marsh paused and looked him squarely in the face. "She needs you, Michael. She's . . . she's sick."

"I don't know what you mean."

"I mean she's very sick. And she doesn't need this . . . disappointment right now on top of everything else." Marsh's voice was rising.

"Oh." Mike dropped his head and shifted his weight to the other foot.

"You already know, don't you? Somebody told you what's wrong with her?"

"I don't know what you're talking about. I know she's in the hospital. She had a nosebleed. That's all I know." Then, "What's the matter with her?"

Marsh, looking straight at Mike, contemplated his answer. There was a long silence. Finally, "She's got leukemia."

Mike's lips parted; no words came out. His eyes swirled from side to side, then focused on Marsh again. "I didn't know."

"Well, you do now."

Marsh turned on his heel, got in his car, and drove away without looking back.

Seventeen

This was the day. Monday morning. Having stopped by to see Randi, Erin arrived at work a few minutes later than usual. Despite the nagging fear of Marsh's reaction, her determination to get the matter out in the open had grown stronger over the weekend.

Freda met her as she came in the front office, asked how Randi was feeling, and volunteered to give blood again if there was a need for more. Erin managed a smile, thanked her, and retreated to her office.

She sat staring at the day's agenda written neatly across her calendar. She needed to reassign two of the employees who'd finished up a project and to evaluate the findings of Ralph's typed project lying on her desk since Tuesday morning. Forty-five more minutes. How could she concentrate? Why had she even bothered to come by here anyway? Why hadn't she done this ten years ago?

She took the folder from the notebook on the walnut shelves and put it beside her purse. Then deciding against that arrangement, she re-inserted the folder and laid the entire notebook by her purse. She wasn't thinking clearly. She couldn't give the reporter the only copy. For the second time, she removed the folder, took out the report, and walked out to the copy machine.

"You want me to do that?" Freda asked.

"No. I'll get it."

Erin picked up each sheet as it fell from the collection rack and cradled it in her arms. Black symbols on white paper. They made all things different. If she could just close her eyes and blot it out forever—as if it had never existed. She remembered college literature courses and class discussions exploring ideas she'd never before considered. Such glimpses of truth, she'd cherished, hid away for later consideration and speculation. The euphoria from such discoveries sometimes lasted days, provided motivation through hours of required research. The report before her represented the antithesis of that feeling.

The last page finished, she returned to her office and closed the door. Taking out a new folder, she placed the copy inside and tucked it underneath her purse again.

Ready.

9:30. She stood up, walked around the room, thought of watering the plants, then shrugged it off. She ambled over to the window and stared out. At least it wasn't rainy or icy; she had no extra energy to expend on driving.

She should have told Marsh before calling the reporter. Would he have encouraged her? Or tried to stop her? Either way, he'd be angry. Every time he came to mind now, she envisioned him with a sullen scowl. She shrank from the image. That wasn't him, was it?

She turned back to the desk and file folder. How would she recognize the reporter? She'd not considered that. The old movies with the man's flower-studded lapel and the woman's white carnation brought a nervous half smile to her lips. She'd know who he was. Weren't all women supposed to have a sixth sense when it came to detecting a man's undue attention? She'd had her share of glances, still attracted attention when she entered a room. Attractive, yes, but she would certainly not call herself glamorous. It was the clothes; everyone appreciated a fashionably dressed woman. She smiled on the days that she'd placed her confidence in her appearance. Only in the last few years had she attributed her success to her abilities.

She thought of the reporter again, a seductive look about his eyes, waiting for her typed treasure. She'd never responded seriously to that look. Frank, one of her immediate supervisors when she'd first joined the company, had been in love with her, lavished her with praise and encouragement at a time when she'd needed both. But so had Marsh, then; he'd easily won.

Admiring men she'd always held at the distance of a working lunch. She smiled at her own naivete and glanced at her watch again. 9:40.

She gathered up the file folder and her purse and headed out the door. I'll be back later," she said as she passed Freda.

Two days lately she'd taken off in the middle of the day. Freda gave her head a slight shake and went back to her typing.

The parking area of the Holiday Inn Coffee Shop looked practically deserted. It was unlikely anyone from town could drive out here on the highway on a fifteen-minute coffee break. Even if she did see someone she knew, she decided that she owed no explanations.

Once inside, she paused by the cashier's booth to let her eyes adjust to the lighting. Two women sat in the booth in the far corner. An older couple in their late sixties sat in the center of the dining room eating pancakes. Back there. The expression around the eyes. A neatly dressed man sat in a booth on the far side.

Erin watched in his direction. As she neared his table, he rose.

"Hello," she spoke. "You're from the *Daily Mirror*?"

"Yes." He extended his hand. "Leon Howard."

"I'm Erin Tilland from Bending and Dowden." She shook his hand, and they sat down. He ordered a second cup of coffee; she declined.

"I'm sorry we couldn't get out here sooner," he offered. "The boss wanted me to cut loose Saturday, but I just couldn't let go of what I was on."

Erin nodded and smiled.

"And getting in and out of here isn't the easiest thing in the world."

"I guess when you're talking about something ten years old, a few days doesn't matter that much." She attempted another smile.

The reporter rubbed his acne-scarred chin, then his forehead with the napkin. He waited with the expression of a ticket holder at a raffle.

"I don't know how much the editor told you. . . ."

"Everything you told him."

"Well, . . . I guess all I need to do is give you the report then." She started to take the papers from the folder, then paused.

"This is . . . it won't be necessary to use my name, will it?"

"No, of course not," the reporter shook his head reassuringly.

She handed the folder to him and watched him read. He read the title page, skimmed the contents, thumbed through the procedures, then intently read the concluding page.

"Hmmm." He turned back to the procedures. He read them through, then leafed through the entire report for the second time before looking up.

"What I need to know, Mrs. Tilland, is why these results were never published before? When they were first made ten years ago?"

"I don't know."

"But you have some idea?"

"No. All I can tell you is that my supervisor then seemed to think they weren't conclusive or important to the public."

"Not conclusive!"

"That's what he said. Of course, our firm was working only on one isolated part of the study in conjunction with other firms. He seemed to think we were only looking at a portion of the project figures—that the government would pull the whole thing together."

"What earlier related research projects was Bending in on?"

"None that I know of."

"You're sure?"

"Yes."

"Who else would likely know?"

"Isaac Morton, maybe."

The reporter jotted down the name.

"But you can't contact him. That'd cause trouble for me. He wouldn't comment anyway."

"Did you read the entire report?"

"Not then. I only read the concluding portion of it and was, of course, upset. But when I asked Mr. Morton about it—the actual dangers—he seemed to brush it off."

"I see."

"I was young, twenty-six, and had just come to work for the company. I didn't know but that he was right. . . . I knew very few of the details or the researchers involved."

"And you never did go in and read the whole thing yourself?"

Erin studied the reporter's face, trying to decide if his tone was accusatory.

"No. I intended to read it when I got a chance. Later that day. But when I went in to look for it again, the report was gone. . . . My daughter was five then." The reporter looked back down at the report while Erin continued, "I was pretty upset about the little bit I had read because . . ."

"This can be verified, can't it?"

"What do you mean?"

"There are other copies somewhere?"

"I would guess the government still has copies."

He was silent again. Then, "No telling which agency has those files now. The way they come and go." He looked up. "Well, you've certainly saved us a lot of time. Handing us a copy like this. No telling how long it would take to sit on somebody's doorstep until they listened to us. Then go through channels to get to somebody who knows something. And once we get to someone with enough authority to let a copy go, we never know if we're getting a straight answer."

Erin nodded. "Then you think it's . . .

significant?"

"It's significant all right." He ran his hand over his hair without disturbing it. "Six times higher risk in this area? Yes, ma'am, it's significant," he repeated. His answers reminded Erin of a doctor's—short but weighty.

"Some big money's going to be involved here," he added.

"My name won't be used, you said?"

"Not if that's the way you want it."

Erin lowered her eyes. Maybe he thought her altruistic for making the leak. She wouldn't accept any commendation from him. Not for something she should have done ten years ago.

She lifted her eyes and looked at him evenly. "When will you run the story?"

"It'll be a few days yet. I'll phone it in, but I'm sure we'll want to recheck some details."

"What details?"

"Actual cases reported. Who was in what position to do what when. Things like that."

Erin's brow furrowed; her lips parted. Every time she'd contemplated Marsh's reaction to the news story, she'd weakened. This past weekend, she'd not allowed herself to think. It was like a fog seen in the distance, something to drive through relying more on instinct than sight. Advance car length by car length. The atmosphere would be clear on the other side.

"Can you imagine what it'd be like," the reporter said aloud more to himself than to her, "to hear your child has leukemia—just because you lived here?"

"Yes, . . ." Erin started to add more, then decided against an explanation that she feared might somehow work its way into the newspaper account. There was a silence; the reporter looked puzzled.

Then, "May I have your phone number?" He took out a pen. She handed him her card.

"Thank you, Mr. . . . ," She couldn't remember his name.

"Howard," he said. "And thank you."

They shook hands; he left the restaurant with his story. Erin sat back down and ordered coffee.

Randi leaned over the back side of the lounge chair and aimed for the wastebasket in the corner of the recreation room, then plopped in a wad of gum wrappers from where she sat. A younger patient, a boy of about twelve, quickly got up, retrieved the wad of paper from its destination, sat back down near Randi, and took a shot himself. He missed.

"Too bad, kid, too bad," Randi teased, then rolled up a sheet of the newspaper lying on the end table and took another shot. The crumpled wad hit the basket for the second time.

"What are you? A basketball player or something?" the young boy asked.

"You're looking at *the one*." Randi bent over in a sweeping bow.

"The one what? You play on a team?"

"Jackson High."

"Oh, no wonder." Bradley wadded up another sheet of newspaper and aimed. Just as he let go of the wad, Erin walked in. She tapped her daughter on the shoulder; Randi spun around.

"You scared me."

"Who were you exepcting?"

"I can go home today."

"What's . . . Has the doctor been by?" Erin looked stunned.

"No. But one of the nurses said that since I was doing so good—better and all—he might let me take the medicine at home."

"She told you that?"

"Yes."

"Well, I don't think she knows exactly what the doctor will do. She shouldn't be telling you that."

"Why not?" Randi sounded irritated. "I asked her if it was possible, and she said 'sometimes.'"

"Well, . . . don't count on it. Until you ask the doctor. I don't think he's going to let you go this soon. They need to get your count up a little higher."

Randi grew quiet, settled back in her chair, and turned to the game show, which had been going in the background. Erin bit her lip; she'd done it again. Why did she always have to see her straight? Burst her bubble? When bubbles were all she had. Insisting that everyone be practical, face the facts—why did she feel that that was her duty in life. She almost loathed herself at the moment.

She wandered around the room a minute, not noticing anything in particular, then sat down across from Randi. They sat quietly for a few minutes, Randi watching the contestants, Erin reliving the morning's meeting. She would have to tell Marsh before the story came out. Maybe tonight.

Erin noted the bright yellow and orange-toned paintings around the lounge walls. They were certainly a contrast to the rooms' decor. Simple sketches requiring little thought. Maybe just being in a cheery atmosphere had lifted Randi's spirits. A cheery atmosphere? Randi would laugh at the idea. But home? The doctor wouldn't let her go home.

"Finally," Dr. Bateman's voice pierced her reverie. "I've been looking all over the place for you. Don't you ever stay in your room?" he smiled and approached them.

Erin stood up, and he spoke to her briefly. He turned back to Randi.

"The nurse tells me you're driving her nuts about going home? You must be feeling better?"

"Yeah. Can I? There's not a patient in here my age."

"You checked it out, huh?"

'She nodded. "Another day in here and I'm going to be climbing the I.V. poles."

"Sounds like real fun to me."

"Can I?"

"I don't know, Randi." he put his hands on

his hips, cocked his head backward, then brushed his mustache from center to tip. "We've still got to keep a close watch on you. That medicine can still take a strange turn."

"I know." Randi patted her stomach.

"How is the nausea?"

"I can take it."

"Good. It should be improving."

"Can I?"

"I don't really think you'd better, Randi." The doctor looked her straight in the eye, folded his arms across his chest. The crow's feet at the corner of each eye softened his expression, gave him a young Marcus Welby look, Erin decided. He continued, "It's so much easier to have you around here to keep a check on things."

Erin was relieved but hoped the feeling didn't show in her face. The thought of having Randi at home where she might have another nosebleed in the night and choke or having her blood count drop too low frightened her.

"Look, I'm old enough to call you, or somebody, and get down here if something happens." Randi's eyes pleaded. "Please? I've already missed almost a week of school. And they're going to get somebody else at Hayden's if I don't hurry and come back. Please?"

The doctor sighed and raised his eyebrows in Erin's direction.

"You'd have to drop by every afternoon at least by 3:00. Let us give you the chemotherapy and observe you for a couple of hours. And you couldn't do anything out of the ordinary until that count comes up. Go to school and come by here. Then go home and rest."

The doctor stood looking at Erin. "What does your mother think?"

Randi's eyes pleaded; she said nothing. Every muscle in Erin's body tensed, and her mind wanted to cry out, to shout no, I can't do it. Instead she heard herself say, "It's okay with me."

Eighteen

Only three or four customers sat in Chessa's Restaurant when Isaac Morton entered and took his usual seat near the doorway. A large man, well over six feet, his gray-plaid business suit fit tightly over his ample chest and stomach. His receding hairline made his large nose all the more prominent. Though not always unwrapped and ready for use, a cigar was a permanent fixture in his hand. The brand name on the side marked its owner as one of the elite of the community.

The waitress, with her hair teased high and heavy rouge, approached his table. "Good morning, Mr. Morton. Here's your coffee."

"Thank you, Hettie. Bring me some sausage this morning with the eggs," he drawled, a lingering trace of the South he'd left behind over thirty-five years ago.

"Okay. Be right back." The waitress didn't bother to write down his order.

Morton pulled out the newspaper he'd picked up from his driveway as he left home earlier that morning. Looking through the local paper quickly, he tossed it aside and got his usual second reading fare from the rack.

The story at the bottom of the first page caught his eye:

LEUKEMIA—FALLOUT LINK SAID KNOWN FOR LAST TEN YEARS

Federal health officials had evidence ten years ago that excessive leukemia and thyroid cancer deaths were occurring in Perry, Unity, and Vale counties here in the state. Residents were exposed to these radioactive materials from U.S. atomic bomb testing done at the above area sites. Officials apparently ignored the findings of their own investigators engaged to study these links. The long-forgotten and unpublished report was obtained this week by investigators for the *Washington Daily Mirror*.

Secretary of the HEW has since ordered the search of other files in the department for related studies. Indeed, two other reports have surfaced which confirm the findings of this document obtained by the *Mirror*.

These studies show that residents of Perry, Vale, and Unity counties were six times more likely to develop leukemia or thyroid cancer as the general population, the most susceptible of the population being young children and teenagers.

Part of the research was conducted through the direction of the Bending and Dowden Company. Local officials of that company reportedly had access to the report's conclusions and failed to bring those findings to the attention of the general public.

Two other existing studies done by other agencies to show links between the fallout and cancer were deemed "inconclusive" and published in recent years. These tests are the ones continually cited by nuclear testing officials as evidence of the safety of the A-Bomb tests.

The *Washington Daily Mirror* is now talking with government officials as to why they suddenly "lost interest" and failed to publish these earlier, contradictory findings. Bending and Dowden will be facing similar questions about their silence. Leukemia and thyroid cancer victims and their families, as well as other area residents, will be eagerly awaiting their answers.

The article continued with details and quotes from three leukemia victims and relatives.

Morton slid the paper under his arm, laid $3 on the table, and started out the door.

"Mr. Morton," Hettie called after him. "We'll

have it ready in a minute. Something wrong?"

"Nothing, Hettie. Don't have time," he said and never changed his gait.

Morton's walk was one that characterized him throughout the Bending and Dowden plant. It was as if one leg spanned yards, and the other reluctantly followed. He strode past the receptionist in the president's office.

"Gardner in?" he asked.

"Yes, he is, Mr. Morton. I'll tell him you're here."

Morton stood frozen in mid-step beside the secretary's desk while she informed her boss he had a visitor. As soon as Gardner answered, Morton burst through his door.

"Have you seen this?" he asked, spreading the paper before his superior.

"Yes." Gardner continued to nod his head up and down, prolonging his answer as if he were going to add more but couldn't yet form the thought into words. His frame was a miniature of Morton's, minus the cigar. But unlike Morton, Gardner's lips turned slightly upward at the corners of his mouth, giving even his solemn expression a softness. Gardner continued, "McElrath has already called. He caught me at home this morning."

"Who else?"

"He and all the councilmen but Richardson. And I may have had a call from him that I've overlooked." Gardner shuffled through the memos scattered across the desk. Then he put his hands in his pockets and paced around to the front of the desk. Taking a few steps back, Morton stood brushing his hand over the remaining patches of gray hair. He turned to face his visitor.

"Who's responsible?"

"I have no idea. No idea." Morton wagged his head.

The president took a long look at him, his eyes narrowed, his mouth screwed to one side. Then the look was gone. Gardner proceeded with his pacing.

"And why now? Why after ten years does somebody get interested in that report?"

Morton wagged his head again and toyed with the cigar.

"Who's wanting to embarrass us?"

"Absolutely no idea. No idea."

"Of course, this radiation issue's in the air. . . . It has been. . . . But this particular study. . . ." Gardner looked up, "You knew about the study?"

"Sure. Sure. I was head of the department then."

"The story's correct, then, about all the findings?"

"As best I remember. But then that was ten years ago. Haven't seen a copy of that report in years. Since I moved out of that building away from those files. Years ago.

"Who has?"

"I can't . . . come up with anybody. Can't come up with anybody."

Gardner stopped his pacing and glared at Morton. There was a long silence.

"The report should've been published when it was made," Gardner said.

"That was up to the government. Their decision, not mine." Morton waved the unlighted cigar. "Up to Uncle Sam, not me."

"You're talking to me, Morton, not the press."

His subordinate averted his eyes and made no reply. Gardner paced back around to the chair behind his desk.

"Any particular reason why you didn't keep me informed about the project when it was being conducted?"

Morton shook his head. "I never thought it was that significant. That was back when they had half a dozen studies going on at the same time. And all of them too small a sampling to mean anything if you ask me."

There was another long silence.

"I'm going to make a statement to the effect that I didn't know such a study existed." He paused. Then, "I can make that statement, Morton. Unfortunately, you can't. . . . And I'm going to order any other related studies be turned over to the investigators. Immediately. . . . Are there any other surprises anywhere?"

Morton shook his head. "Not that I know of. No, not that I know of."

"People out there are going to be angry enough to rip this place apart. And I don't blame them."

"I don't know about that. You know that sometimes the reaction . . ."

"They will be," Gardner cut him off. "Anybody who comes to you, you refer them to me. I don't want you to say anything to anybody."

Morton turned and stalked out of the office faster than his normal gait.

"Here are a couple other messages." The secretary handed the yellow notes to her boss through the opened door after Morton's departure. Gardner released them to flutter to his desktop to join the already cluttered pile.

Nineteen

Erin made her own discovery of the headlines. Although the reporter had told her Monday that the story would not be out for another two or three days, she hadn't been able to rest. Randi, not in the habit of looking at the paper, would not notice until someone called her attention to the article. But she couldn't put off telling Marsh any longer.

She'd intended to tell him Monday night, but then Randi had come home from the hospital. It just didn't seem the appropriate time. Even if Randi had been out of the house, out of earshot.

Erin had gotten up at six but had been awake since 4:30 contemplating how best to tell him. Story or not, she had to tell him today.

Marsh had been called out in the middle of the night and had come home late. She was awake when he'd crawled in bed beside her, but she had not let him know. She had proven very deft at "sleeping" through such late night interruptions. Another thing about their marital pattern that had not always been so. During her back-to-college days, most of their talking had taken place at such odd hours of the night. Marsh, the light sleeper, would always wake up when she crawled into bed after studying late. Or, often, returning from the library after its midnight closing hour, she'd find him still waiting up for her. He'd heat water and bring her a cup of hot tea or coffee while she stored away note cards and books and organized her papers for the next day. Then he'd follow her into the bedroom and help her undress. They'd gradually find themselves in bed. After making love, she, often preoccuppied with an upcoming exam or paper, found sleep eluded her. Snuggling closer to him, she'd ask if he was asleep, knowing that the sound of her voice would wake him. He'd rouse, and they'd discuss her upcoming assignment or whatever and then move on to another topic until she talked her way to sleep. It was as if she held all her words in check during the day to pour them out to her sole confidant at night.

But as she'd grown more confident in her career, she'd needed to lean on his advice less. He, contrarily, growing unhappier in his job as it leveled to a plateau, needed to talk—to vent his frustrations. Erin listened, sympathetically at first, then dutifully, to the same complaints over and over. When she felt he was being unreasonable, she said so. He recoiled, withdrew completely. When she failed to be his accomplice in complaint, he tagged her an adversary. Maybe she'd let him down. The late-night sharing had grown more infrequent. They simply made love and slept.

At 6:00 Erin slipped out of bed, put on robe and slippers, and went out to get both papers from the yard. There on the bottom of page one she read the headline: "Leukemia-Fallout Link Said Known for Last Ten Years."

As she read the article, her eyes glided along, devouring every word, considering its connotations and ramifications. She reread the paragraph about their company's releasing the reports before laying the paper aside to prepare Randi's breakfast.

After getting Randi off to school, she sat reading the story again, laying the paper aside for reflection, then re-reading it again. And again. And again. Marsh would be up shortly. She'd wait.

She heard the shower running, then the electric razor. Maybe she should go on in the bedroom where he was. No, she'd wait in here. She sat staring out the breakfast-nook window, watching nothing in particular. A cobweb between the curtain and rod. Younger kids passing by on bicycles. Two lone pink roses. The sunshine promised a beautiful May day.

"I thought you'd already gone to work," Marsh said as he entered the kitchen.

He wore a baby blue shirt and pants, Erin's favorite color. He used to wear blue to please her; now he wore it absent-mindedly. Erin looked at her own zip-up-the-front velour robe. She always hated to argue, to make him angry when she looked so frowsy. She knew the fear stemmed from the thought that he might find solace elsewhere. She glanced back out the window. Cool, crisp breeze blowing. Bright sunshine. He matched the spring morning, not her mood.

"Are you sick?" he asked.

"No."

He shrugged, sauntered over to the cabinet, and took out a box of cereal.

"Do you want me to fix you some toast?"

"No."

She watched him a moment longer. His blond hair always neatly trimmed cupped the tips of his ears. It was always the first thing she noticed about him, a barometer telling her if he'd been in his office all day or had taken the afternoon off to play tennis. She wanted to have him sit down in a chair, feel his arms around her, dig her fingers into his hair, bury his face against her. She couldn't.

"Marsh, I want to talk to you."

"Okay."

"I talked to a reporter Monday morning."

He took a bowl from the cabinet and poured his cereal. Being used to reading newspaper accounts of the company's findings, he didn't understand the import of her words. Local opinion polls, new-product research, effects of various advertising campaigns all periodically found their way into print. He looked at Erin rather impatiently, still waiting for the reason this particular meeting should have significance for him.

"Here." She held the folded section of the newspaper toward him. "Read this."

"Just a minute." Instead of reaching for the paper, he opened the refrigerator for the milk.

"It's about leukemia."

Marsh set the bowl down, took the paper from her, and read. She searched his face for reaction; he was expressionless.

"Our researchers found the link," Erin said after a minute.

"That's what it says." Marsh laid the paper down and walked over to the window. He stood gazing out into the sunshine, seeing nothing. For a long time, neither spoke.

Then Marsh turned around to face her. "You gave them the story?"

Erin nodded. "I'm head of that department now."

"But you weren't then . . . when they did the study?"

"No . . ." Erin swallowed, struggled to add the significant statement, "but I knew about the study when it was done. I saw the final report ten years ago."

"You knew about it when it was made?" Marsh's face contorted, and his hands came out of his pockets. "You knew this all along and yet you never, you never . . . even . . . you insisted we stay here anyway in this . . . this deathtrap?"

210

Erin stood staring at him, eyes searching, pleading for compassion she no longer was sure he could give. Tears did not come at all.

"How could you . . ." Marsh's voice grew huskier now, "how could you just . . . stay here and . . . kill your own daughter?"

"Marsh!"

"You did. You honestly did. If I'd had my way, we'd have left here a long time ago. It was your job, your school, your life. . . . Randi and me, what do we count for?" His voice came hoarsely at a sporadic cadence.

"Marsh, please . . . please try to understand."

"What's to understand? My God, Erin, tell me what's to understand?"

"I didn't think . . ."

"Didn't think?" Marsh cut her off. "Didn't think? How could you help but think? With that report in black-and-white right under your nose?"

"But I didn't think it could happen to us. I just . . ."

"What about the rest of the world? Did you ever give a thought to anybody else besides yourself?"

"Of course, I did. But the government supervised the study. I kept thinking . . . Mr. Morton said if they were sure—if the findings were significant—the government would release them."

"They didn't."

"I know that now. . . . Marsh, try to understand what I'm saying. How I felt." She walked around in front of him again. He turned away. "Listen to me."

Marsh stood frozen with teeth clenched; Erin dropped her hands from his shoulders as if they'd been yanked away.

"When you read something like that, . . . you don't ever know what to think. What to do at the time."

"*You* might not."

"All right. All right," she yelled. "*I* might not. *I* didn't think. *I* didn't know what to do." She paused, lowered her voice to normal level. "People know smoking causes cancer, but they keep on smoking."

"That's their choice. They're adult, Erin. We're talking about submitting a child, a helpless child who hasn't an idea . . ." he didn't finish, but rather stood clenching his fists together and then apart.

"What I meant was that you—people just don't think it will happen to them—that it will really happen at all."

Marsh glared into her face for a long time before turning away again to the window. Erin stood motionless in the same spot, watching her husband at the window. She understood how he could blame her when she'd gone through the same fear, rage, and helpless sinking feeling he was now experiencing. He had every right to feel as he did. Yet she could not help but hope for compassion, if not understanding.

For what seemed like hours, Erin stood in the

center of the kitchen. The blue and gold diametrically-patterned couch, the matching chair, the beautifully-framed pictures, the glass and wrought-iron dinette exuded an atmosphere of cozy comforts in a house where there was none.

Marsh headed for the door.

"Where are you going?"

"I don't know."

"What can I do? Tell me what I can do or say?"

"Nothing you can ever do matters anymore." Marsh strode on through the back door toward his car.

Erin hesitated a moment, then followed him out. He yanked open the car door and started to climb in.

"Is that all you know how to do? Walk out? Be dramatic?"

He slammed the door closed, dropped his head. He draped his elbow off the top of the car, the other arm rested on his hip. She stared at the top of his head, watched as his body shifted positions, weight moving from one foot to the other, leaning forward, then backward. His head turned first to the left, then the right, as if he were debating with himself. He slowly dropped his elbow from the cartop and walked back into the house leaving more than ample clearance between himself and Erin.

He slumped into a dinette chair, went limp. Erin walked back to the bar and stood facing him, saying nothing.

They waited.

The atmosphere felt thick, stifling to Erin. What was there to say? Did nothing really matter? His last words seemed to ricochet off the walls.

"Do you want to quit, Marsh?" she asked aloud.

He looked up, searching her eyes for meaning. He understood.

"Why didn't you tell me?" His tone was child-like, pained.

"I was afraid you'd react . . . just like you did, blame me."

He slammed his fist into the table. "What did you expect me to say? 'How interesting. What's for dinner?'"

"Can't you talk without being sarcastic?"

"Yes, I can talk without being sarcastic," he shot out in one breath. Then silence.

"Why is it always me, Marsh? Why am I always the villain. The . . . the intruder?"

He didn't answer.

She continued, "I'd have moved if you'd have insisted."

"Sure you would have."

"I would have. Did you forget all the moves before here? . . . You agreed on staying. Liked the mountains, your job."

"I didn't know what you knew."

"I didn't either then." She was losing the thread of the conversation. It was too complicated to untangle.

Silence.

"Marsh, it's not just Randi."

"What's not just Randi?"

"The problem."

"Which problem?"

"Our problem. She's just your weapon. It's your problem." Marsh sneered. Erin continued, "You're unhappy with yourself, your job, feel insecure."

"Is that what analyist Erin thinks? That I'm a weird, frustrated nobody, taking it out on the world? Is that what she thinks?"

"I didn't say that." Erin lowered her eyes. She hated the cold stare, the rage in his voice.

"Then what did you say?"

"Nothing. Drop it."

"Now, look who won't talk. I'm always walking out, you say. Clam up, walk out, what's the difference?"

She said nothing, turned her back to him. He stood up, caught her shoulder, and swung her around to face him. "What do you want? What do you expect me to feel?" He asked, prodded, pleaded, demanded all at the same time, his tone changing with each word.

Erin hesitated, looking him straight in the eye. What did she want? Ultimately? Now, at this moment? "I want to be a part of your life, Marsh. And a part of Randi's. I want you to be happy so you can let me be happy. . . . I want you to let Randi get near me. . . ."

"I'm not keeping Randi . . ."

"I want you to love me again, Marsh." She blinked back the tears.

He withdrew his hands from her shoulders.

His glare vanished; his eyes softened.

"I do love you."

"You don't, Marsh. You don't. You need me, but you don't love me anymore. You hate yourself for needing me even.

He turned away and walked to the window again. The sun hung higher in the morning sky. Neighbors were stirring, leaving for work, gathering in the morning paper, letting their dogs out. He watched the activity, conscious of none.

"Do you want a divorce?"

"You should have told me, Erin." His words crept out of his mouth this time, edged toward her. "I can't forget that."

He turned and walked out the door. She let him go.

Twenty

Although not the same to the personnel in the Research Division as it was to the men in the tinted-glass buildings across the street, the news story, nevertheless, drew odd reactions.

Ralph and Freda stood in the office hallway discussing the matter as other employees came drifting through one by one to get coffee.

"Well, now we know why Buglione is the size he is," Ralph said, slapping a co-worker on the shoulder as he passed between them.

"What's this?" Buglione paused for the punch line.

"That's why you're 6'8" and going on 300."

"240's bad enough. Let's not make it any worse than it is. And I bet you can't even tell I've lost ten pounds?"

"No kidding. Where?" Ralph asked.

"Right here, Ralph," Freda said, patting the twenty-three year old's protruding stomach.

"Atta girl. I knew somebody noticed."

"Wife making you lose it?" Ralph asked.

Buglione grinned. "And why are we standing here at this hour of the morning discussing my weight and marital situation?"

"Don't you read the papers?"

"Not if I can help it."

"Thyroid. We're talking about your thyroid. It's gone wild, Buglione. No telling when you might stop growing."

"What are you talking about?"

"They're telling us that living here in these wide open spaces with your beautiful snow-covered mountains and your green fertile valleys," Ralph's tone grew more theatrical, "is going to do us in."

"Come on, . . ." Buglione raised his eyebrows and looked at Freda. "What's he talking about?"

Ralph continued, "There's an article in the paper this morning saying we're all walking time-bombs. Walking around with hidden leukemia or thyroid cancer because we've been breathing the radiation in the air."

"What radiation?"

"From the nuclear testing sites."

"They're not doing that around here anymore, are they?"

"Not now, they aren't," Freda interrupted.

"When you were a kid, Buglione. You were a little kid once, weren't you?"

"I didn't live here. Moved here two years ago."

"Oh." Ralph snapped his fingers. "Then

you'll have to pay a doctor bill to find out what your weight problem is."

Buglione grew serious. "Why are they just now telling people about it?"

"And get sued?" Ralph asked. "No, they've had ten years now to muddy the water and lay the blame somewhere else."

"Ten years ago and just now printing the story?"

"They didn't know there was a story then," Freda answered.

"Yeah, that's the real kicker," Ralph added. "And guess who handled the research?"

"No kidding?" Buglione let go a low half-whistle.

"No kidding."

"Somebody's going to be under fire."

"Don't you know it," Freda added.

"Pays to be a nobody around here, doesn't it?" Ralph slapped Buglione on the back again. The younger man walked on down the hall to get coffee.

"Well, all I can say is I hope everybody is in as jolly-good mood as you are about the whole thing," Freda said to Ralph.

"What's to do about it now? If you got it, you got it. When it's your time, it's your time."

Freda grinned and bobbed on off toward the next group of employees huddled down the hallway.

Erin, despite a few days' warning, was still not up to the confrontations she feared might be coming when the story broke. Gloria had called and caught her just as she was leaving for work. Fuming about the situation, she'd kept Erin on the phone fifteen minutes answering questions about what she thought the government planned to do.

Once in the office, Erin found a note on her desk saying that Isaac Morton wanted her to drop by his office "at her earliest possible convenience." Because Morton was no longer responsible for the work coming through her office, his request that she drop by came as a surprise. Actually, he was no longer in a position to "request" her coming by. Their minimal involvement in the last couple years hardly included more than an exchange of temporary personnel.

Erin walked into Morton's office, her generally confident manner gone. This conference, she knew, did not concern approbation of her work.

"Well, Erin, how are you?" Morton came around to the front of the desk and stretched out his hand.

"Fine, thank you, Isaac. And you?"

"Fine, fine. It's been a while since we've talked. Quite a while. You must have a handle on that place. I don't hear much from your side of the street when things are going smoothly."

"True." Erin nodded. "In that case, no news is good news. Isn't that what they keep saying?" Erin glanced around the office noting only one familiar painting, which he'd transferred from his old office. The color scheme, browns and blacks, was completely different in the newer buildings, definitely more masculine.

"I don't think I've been in your new office before."

"Oh, surely you have. Surely you have."

"No. I don't think so. I think most of our conversations have been over the phone. Anyway, I like the decor over here—throughout the building."

"Well, I didn't have much say about it. They had it almost completely furnished when I moved in."

Erin noted the two wilted potted plants, obviously his additions. He'd had to replace green plants around his office across the street as often as typewriter ribbons.

"Well, sit down. Sit down." Morton just seemed to notice that they were still standing. He pulled a chair for Erin around closer to the desk.

"I guess you've seen the story?" Morton asked.

"Yes, I have."

"Who hasn't, may be the more appropriate question."

Erin couldn't read Morton's attitude—whether he suspected her of the leak and how upset he was. Certainly Jarvis, her immediate predecessor, who'd recently left the company, should be the more likely suspect. Even though Morton and she mutually appreciated each other's capabilities, they'd never been friends.

Morton continued after a moment's hesitation. "I've been in to talk to Gardner earlier this morning. He's issuing a statement that he knew nothing about the study's ever having been done. And he wants all related reports handed over to the investigators—the papers, the government, or whoever—immediately. Do you know of any others tucked away in the files?"

"No, I don't."

He paused again, straightened himself in the chair and leaned forward. After a moment he ambled around, hoisted his shorter leg up, and took a seat on the edge of the desk beside Erin's chair.

"What I'd like to know is how some reporter got a hold of that report."

Erin swallowed and lifted her head slightly. "From me."

"You." He drawled his response, more a statement than a question.

"Yes."

"I thought so."

"Why?"

Morton shrugged. A smile of condescension.

"Didn't you consider Jarvis?"

"Not really."

"Why not?"

"He's been gone too long. If he'd have come across it and intended to do something about it, we'd have already heard from him. Before he got out the door good." Morton paused and looked directly into Erin's face. "No, Erin, I figured it was you."

She sat poised, waiting for his explanation,

refusing to throw accolades for his perceptiveness by an amazed expression.

"Still see your face that first morning you saw it. The report. Talked to me about it. Scared half to death." Morton grinned and relaxed his gaze on her. Then, "I expected something from you then."

Erin looked away.

He continued, "But why now? Why this way? Why didn't you let someone know you were going to do it? We could have looked like heroes instead of . . ." he didn't finish.

"Do you honestly think Gardner would've approved release if I had?"

Morton made no response, examined his cigar ceremoniously.

Then, "Well, Erin. I'm . . . relieved."

"Relieved?"

"To know. For sure." He tapped his cigar on the ashtray. "I expected the story."

"Why?"

"Strange phone call over the weekend. Smelled like some reporter. I can smell one a mile away. Dodging in and out my questions. Course, I denied everything, but I figured he had a story anyway before he ever called."

Erin made no reply.

"But why? I could have understood your doing it when you first saw the report. Young. A baby to protect. I felt . . . outraged myself about all the lies we'd been told. Still am. But . . ." he raised his arm in a sweeping gesture, "but why now?" Erin's eyes clouded.

Then, "This bothering you?" He held out his cigar toward her.

She shook her head. Morton leaned back away from her, puffed again, then slowly exhaling, studied her face.

"My daughter has leukemia."

"I'm . . . sorry."

Morton took the cigar out of his mouth, looked away, stood up, and walked over to the swivel chair and stood with his back to her.

Erin studied his large frame. *I'm sorry*—is that what people said when you told them your daughter might be dying? Morton turned abruptly and returned to sit down in the same spot on the side of the desk. His face was as expressionless as if Erin had commented on the weather.

"I guess you know what kind of PR job this is going to take."

Erin swallowed hard, set her jaw, felt the hollow of her cheek ripple. "The government had the jurisdiction and the responsibility to publish the findings as soon as the study was done. Public reaction should be directed toward them," she said.

"Oh, it will be—nationally," he assured her with a wave of the cigar. "The local picture is going to be something else." He gazed toward the window. "We're sitting here in everybody's backyard. They're going to look at this like uncovering a murder weapon and then waiting for the officials to come ask us if we found it."

"I wish I'd done it ten years ago," Erin said,

staring past Morton, who still sat studying her face as if to detect some further motive for the leak. "Shall I go directly to Gardner and tell him where the story came from?"

"No." Morton snapped to attention. "Not unless he asks. If I were you, I'd just sit tight. Sit tight." Morton leaned over closer to her. "Why don't you let me take care of it for you?"

"That's . . . thoughtful of you Isaac, but . . ."

"I'll tell him about your daughter, and he'll . . ."

"I think I'll go to Gardner myself." She stood up.

"You sure could make trouble for yourself." He shook his cigar at her. "No, I wouldn't do that. I don't think he'd think too highly of leaking such information without prior approval from him."

"No, he probably won't, Isaac." She turned toward the door.

"Wait a minute. Look at this from both angles." He spoke slowly now, his tone cordial again. "I'm going to look bad because I didn't call it to his attention when the study was done. You look bad because you threw it to the dogs without getting his approval."

"We both made our mistakes ten years ago."

Morton followed her to the door. "I don't really think he'll ever press the issue. In fact, he seemed almost glad this morning that the story was out. Humanitarian sort of guy, he is. I don't think he's going to be too upset if he never learns who handed it over."

"Good. That'll make it a little easier when I talk to him."

Erin walked on out the door. Morton stood in the doorway puffing his cigar and watched her go.

Once around the corner, Erin stopped and leaned against the building directory map on the corridor wall. The pulse in her temples throbbed. Her mouth felt like cotton. She stared at the names on the map, already knowing its contents well. A ripple went through her body; she took it off and walked on down the hall to Mr. Gardner's suite.

"I need to talk to Mr. Gardner, please."

"I'm sorry; he's awfully busy this morning. Perhaps I could make an appointment for you tomorrow." The secretary sounded canned.

"I'd like to talk to him about the newspaper story." Erin's voice was barely audible.

"I see. Well, why don't you come on back here and have a seat. I'll tell him you're here."

The secretary disappeared behind Gardner's door and then returned to show Erin into his office.

"Yes, Erin. What can I do for you?" Then, "Excuse me, please have a seat," Gardner gestured toward the couch. "One of those mornings. I'm sure you've seen the paper."

"Yes."

"Of course. That's what my secretary said you wanted to see me about." Gardner shrugged as if embarrassed at his absent-mindedness. Erin noted the up-turned corners of his mouth, despite the solemn glare of his eyes. She was glad he, rather than Morton, held her job in his hands. She sat up straight on the edge of the couch and slowly drew in her breath before speaking.

"The *Daily Mirror* got the copy of the radiation research findings from me." The words sprang from her almost without warning.

Gardner, still standing, leaned forward and rested his hands on the desktop. He stared at her. "Why?"

"I thought the public had a right to know."

"Did you just now come across the report in the files?"

"No . . . ten years ago. I saw the report on Isaac Morton's desk ten years ago."

"But why didn't you discuss it with me first? I didn't even know the study existed." Gardner sat down behind the desk and waited.

"I'm sorry," her voice grew firmer, and she shifted her rigid position on the sofa. "I should have told somebody then. But I . . . kept thinking the government would make a statement if the reports were significant—I didn't get a chance to read all the report, only the recommendations and conclusions. I kept waiting. And waiting. The months kept dragging by with no word. I . . ."

"But why didn't you come to me before you released it?" His tone grew sharp for the first time during their conversation.

"I guess I thought I . . . our firm wouldn't . . . would look bad for waiting this long. . . . I thought we wouldn't be mentioned in the newspaper article this way."

Gardner still stared at her.

"I thought they'd lay the whole thing at the government's doorstep. It was their project to begin with."

The president turned his pencil end over end. "It's certainly going to cause us some embarrassment. . . . And that's a mild term for the reaction I've had this morning."

"I guess I assumed that if I came to you or some other official first, the story would be filed away again."

"Certainly not." Gardner's face reddened. "I knew nothing at all about the project when it was done. It should've been published long ago. . . . If I'd known about it, it would have."

Erin was quiet while Gardner stared down at his desktop and continued to slide his pencil through his fingers.

"You can bet there'll be some lawsuits," he said.

"Against us?"

"I don't know. Maybe. Against the government most likely. They wouldn't have a leg to stand on suing us."

He ran his hand through his white hair, still as full and thick as when Erin had first met him. He shook a handful of telephone messages in her direction. "Everyone from the mayor on down to dog catcher has called for an explanation and/or lecture. You'd think we were responsible for the nuclear tests rather than just investigating the damage. People want to blame somebody—anybody they can see. . . . The government's too big to tear apart; we're not."

"I'm sorry. I . . . I just couldn't play hide-and-seek any longer."

"But you still haven't explained why, now, you decided to bring this to light?"

Thinking of Morton's earlier reaction, she waited, considered, weighed her words.

"My daughter has leukemia, Mr. Gardner."

"I see." There was a long pause. Then, "I'm sorry. Was she just diagnosed?"

"A few months ago."

"Is she in remission yet?"

"She had one remission. Then she lost it a couple weeks ago."

"I'm sorry," he said again, then looked away. Silence.

"I only mentioned it to say that we—I—was part of the public 'out there' that we keep mentioning who will have to live with our decision to remain silent all these years."

"Now wait a minute. You sound like some of these people who've been calling. You have to remember that it wasn't our doing that got us into this—that put the radiation in the air. Caused the hazard."

"I'm only saying that if people had known about the danger, they could have left the area."

"You didn't."

"I know that." Erin looked away. "I know

that, and I'll continue to know that for the rest of my life."

Both were silent for a few minutes. Gardner rose and walked over to the large picture window overlooking the courtyard to the south. She could see portions of the landscape jutting out from around the edges of his short, stocky frame. The roof of her own office building extended in the background beyond the courtyard trees. Her earlier days as secretary for Bending and Dowden came to mind. She recalled people's faces she'd worked with as if examining an old photo album. The mistakes she'd made, the recriminations. Then the important projects, the praise from Mr. Gardner himself. Their last few years together. His even asking her advice from time to time in administrative meetings. Gardner kept his back to her and continued gazing out the window for a long time.

Erin broke the silence, her voice calmly under control, "Do you want my resignation?"

He made no move or attempt to speak. Clutching her purse in front of her, she stood motionless in the center of the office. She felt numb, every muscle of her body completely balanced against an opposing one. She gazed at the president's profile, as if they both were marble statues adding to the decor. It was as if any effort to blink her eyes, to shift her purse from one hand to the other, to step forward or backward would affect her equilibrium. So she stood. It was almost over.

He turned and faced her. "No, Erin. I'll not make any further explanations to the press than what I've already made."

"Thank you," came out almost as a whisper. She turned and left his office.

Twenty-One

Marsh rolled over on his office couch and gazed at the ceiling, so familiar after a night's insomnia. He hadn't been home since leaving Erin the morning before. Hospital personnel banged and clanged in the halls, moving equipment from one area to another. What day was it? Thursday. He was off today. He had to get up and get out.

The phone buzzed. On the eighth ring Marsh lifted the receiver to his ear, but said nothing.

"Marsh? You there?"

"Yes."

"Mark Templar. I'm sorry to bother you so early. Somebody said they thought you spent the night here."

Marsh held the phone, saying nothing. Many nights he'd spent at the hospital waiting for families to hear news about some loved one. Last night and yesterday had been his own emergency.

"I'm here," he said flatly.

"Can you meet me on the second floor? I've got to tell a young man his wife has just died."

Every fiber within him cringed and cried out no. He ran his hand across his bearded face and glanced distractedly at his wrinkled shirt and pants. He hung up the phone without answering the doctor.

"Thanks for coming," Templar said, as Marsh stepped off the elevator on the second floor. "It looks like you've been around here a while?"

Marsh nodded.

"Well, I'm glad you were around. I couldn't have waited for you on this one. The family's already here."

Marsh walked alongside the doctor down the corridor.

"They came in about 4:30 this morning. Car accident. Husband didn't have a scratch, but his wife was in bad shape. Couldn't help her."

The doctor turned and directed Marsh on down the hall toward the waiting room near Surgery. As they approached, a short, stocky man about twenty-two rose and came toward them, followed by an older couple in their fifties.

The doctor shook hands with the young man and his in-laws, then turned to introduce

Marsh. "This is Reverend Tilland, the chaplain here at Memorial."

A wild look of fear came into the young man's eyes. Marsh noted the faint tremor which went through the man's body as they shook hands. He hated it. It was as if patients and families mistook him for the misfortune threatening to destroy their world.

At the doctor's suggestion, the young man and the older couple sat down.

"I'm sorry, Doug, Mr. and Mrs. Sedell. There was nothing we could do." The doctor's voice continued, but Marsh tuned out the explanations about the extent of the injuries and what they had tried to do in surgery. Instead, his attention focused on the face of the three sitting before him. The younger man, the husband, held his head in his hands and wept openly.

The doctor's voice stopped. He rose to go.

"Reverend Tilland will be here with you for a while. And please feel free to get in touch with me a little later if you have any questions. . . . I'm sorry," he repeated. The doctor clasped the older man's hands, then patted the younger's shoulder and walked away.

Marsh stared at the family in front of him. So many times, he'd waited with a grieving family to let them vent their anger, to come to accept the reality of death. To gather themselves together enough to leave the hospital. Now it was as if he faced such a family for the first time.

He had nothing to offer them. Instead, he sat as one waiting to be comforted himself.

Two orderlies passed the waiting room entrance pushing what looked like an empty stretcher. Then a maid came through with her cleaning cart. Both waited for the elevator and then disappeared. The area grew quiet again where the four sat. The smell of rubbing alcohol and cleaning disinfectant lingered in the air.

"Is there something I can do?" Marsh heard himself ask. The husband lifted his face and stared at him blankly.

"She was our only daughter," Mrs. Sedell said, tears streaming down her face.

Marsh stared; words would not come.

"I did it; I was driving," the husband began to explain to him in a broken voice between sobs. "But I didn't mean to." He rocked from side to side in his chair. "I didn't mean to. We . . . we were just leaving early . . . to get a head start to get home to see my folks for the weekend." The husband seemed determined to get the explanation out.

"I see." Marsh nodded.

"My parents didn't even know we were coming. We were going to get there by breakfast and surprise them when they got up." It seemed to be important to the young man that Marsh fully understand the situation. "That's why we had to leave so early. But she didn't want to get up and I made her. She likes to sleep in and she never gets to and I made her get up, I just . . . the rain . . ." his voice trailed off again, and he lowered his head.

Marsh turned to the parents again. The older man's arm cradled his wife; she was crying softly now.

"Do you have . . . do they have children?"

"No, thank the Lord. It'd be too much on a child to lose a mother," Mr. Sedell's statement took Marsh by surprise. So frequently he heard parents lamenting the fact that they had no grandchild to remember the deceased by.

"Is there someone else you should notify?" Marsh's voice was flat.

"Not yet," the mother answered. "Doug'll want to call his folks himself. . . . It's just such a shock. . . . When Doug called about 5:00 to tell us . . . they had had an accident . . . it was like a . . . dream. I can't really believe we're here. That it's happening."

"Why?" the young husband asked, raising his head. His wet face glistened; he waited for Marsh to answer.

Why? Why? Were they asking why? They were asking him.

"Why?" the husband repeated. "What have we ever done to deserve this? Twenty-three. She was only twenty-three."

Is he still asking? Marsh leaned forward. The older man reached out and patted Marsh's knee.

The explanations Marsh had always given

continued to roll through his mind. In the past, he would have tried to answer that God didn't "do this" to them, that He gave man his own free will to exercise, to make choices, to make mistakes, to drive too fast, to whatever it was that caused the problem. He might have answered that some things happen due to sin in the world—the evil design of Godless creatures reeking havoc on unsuspecting victims. Or that God had set natural laws in motion; they couldn't be stopped without chaos. Or that God's ways are mysterious—that why He doesn't intervene to prevent tragedy can't be understood in this world.

The chaplain recalled all these answers. But he gave none.

The older man spoke to his son-in-law. "That's where a man's faith comes in, Doug."

The young man leaned forward out of his chair and knelt in front of his in-laws on the sofa facing him.

"I didn't mean to do it," he sobbed into the mother-in-law's lap. "I'm so sorry."

The woman stroked the blond hair strung out on her lap; her husband patted the son-in-law's shoulder.

Marsh sat observing the scene as if he were watching a movie on a faraway drive-in screen. The sound faded; the movement grew hazy.

"Call me anytime."

He lifted his heavy body from the chair and walked from the room.

* * *

Back in his office, Marsh bent over the sofa bed, collected the blanket, and stuffed it into the top of the closet. Then gathering his tie and jacket from the doorknob, he opened the door to leave.

Where was he going? He eased the door closed, backed up and sat down. Alternatives raced through his mind; each in turn, rejected. Where do people go when they're no longer able to function as capable people? When they can no longer fill the capacity they've trained for all their live? When they're completely empty, void, nothing, non-existent emotionally and intellectually? Marsh couldn't answer his well-formed questions.

He felt like a machine whose inner mechanism had been set in motion and left to run on automatic without the aid of mental intervention. Where could he go to run this racing mechanism down, to stop the whirl, to rest until his mind could catch up to the routine?

He'd been used. Erin had known about the report all along. Kept it from him intentionally. Ashamed of the truth. She'd used them—he and Randi—like burning logs to keep her career afire.

A change of mood came over him. His drained, blank facial expression took on a tensed appearance. The pupils in his eyes dilated. His jaw locked into a scowl. He stood up from the couch, stalked out of his office, and drove home. Once there, he undressed, showered, dressed again. Then he pulled a bag out of the hall closet. It was the one Erin always used when traveling. Tossing it aside, he got the larger one and closed the closet. He paused to pick up the first bag and put it away, then set it back down, leaving it exactly in the middle of the hallway. She couldn't miss it. He packed the larger bag quickly and left the house.

Pulling into Moody Park, he eased the car slowly up near the tennis courts. Two small girls rode their bikes through the narrow passageway between the car and the fenced-off courts. Other than the older man sitting on the park bench near the highway, the birds and a squirrel were the only inhabitants of this small, out-of-the-way park. The two cracked tennis courts, generally empty, had long-past rendered their service to the community.

Marsh sat in the car for a long while, staring out the window at the passing cars at least a hundred yards in front of him. Then relaxing his grip on the steering wheel, he retrieved his tennis racket and bucket of balls from the floorboard and headed toward the courts. Just inside the fenced-in area, he spattered the first ball against the backboard and missed the return as the ball sailed past him. He threw the second ball into the air and repeated the process. Then the third and the fourth and the fifth. Again and again and again, he slammed the balls, not bothering for the return.

Having exhausted his supply, he gathered up the balls and began the process again. Then, after sending several buckets-full toward the wooden board, he stopped the routine as suddenly as he'd begun it. He walked closer to the board, tossed the ball in the air, then returned it to the board with a steady, even swing. Stretching, bending, leaning, grasping, racing forward, leaping back, dashing sideways. Occasionally he dropped the racket to the ground, raced full speed to the other end of the courts to collect the balls lying around the area. Returning to position, he began the process again. Up, back, sideways, extending his arm high above his head, withdrawing it to catch a close side-grazing one, lunging to the left, then the right. Again. Again. Again.

He dropped to the grass beside the water fountain. The older man, long-forgotten since Marsh took the court, made his way over to where Marsh lay exhausted beneath the midmorning sun.

"Gettin' a little exercise, huh?" The old man, dressed in khaki slacks and plaid shirt, stopped a few yards from where Marsh lay and stood with his thumbs hooked over his pants' pockets.

Marsh continued to breathe deeply and nodded.

"You must be in good shape, Bud," the older man spoke again. "To keep at it like you was doing."

Marsh continued the deep-breathing routine.

"I used to be able to do that. Course, tennis wasn't a fad in them days like it is now. Nobody paid no attention to how you played the game."

Marsh eyed the man's frame, stooped shoulders gently rounded now, legs slightly bent at the knees, hands and fingers crippled with arthritis. The man's ruddy complexion, spotted with scaly patches of skin, called attention to the wrinkles set in by too many years on outside park benches, or tennis courts as the old man would probably have it.

Marsh rolled over and looked up. He made a slight groan. That was the only response the old man needed to continue the one-sided conversation. "You come out here much?"

Marsh shook his head.

"Didn't think so. Most people already found them better courts somewhere. I sit right over there pretty near every day, and I never seen you. Course, I don't catch everything what goes on around here." The man chuckled. "But I do like to watch a good tennis player. I got a great granddaughter. She's twelve. They don't get to come too often, but when her folks come down, I bring her out here. She and the boy, her kid brother. They make quite a pair on the courts. Fight. You oughta see them kids argue about them boundary lines." The man pointed to faint white lines around the courts. "Why you can't see 'em half way around even in the daylight. Much less at night." The man chuckled louder this time. "You got kids?"

"A daughter."

"How old?"

"Sixteen."

"Well, you know 'bout a kid's energy, don't you? . . . Yep, great place to bring up kids—out here in this part of the country. Brought up all four of mine out here. Healthy as horses. They need a chance to get out in the open. Good for the soul, ain't it?" The old man shaded his eyes with his hand for a moment, looked around, then rehooked it on his pocket. "Good Lord sure knows how to take care of us, don't He? Good weather. These mountains."

Marsh stared straight ahead. The old man took a step backward, looked off a moment, then turned back.

"You believe in a God?" the old man asked.

Marsh stared at him, his eyes narrowed. Finally, "I think."

"Well . . . now that's a different twist. Most people, you ask them that and they come right out with a powerful feeling. Either they preach you a sermon or they claim they don't put no store in such foolishness."

Marsh made no response.

"My wife's like that. Ain't got time to waste on such notions, she claims. . . . You married?"

"Yes."

"You thought about it much?" the old man

asked after a moment.

"What?"

"A God?"

Marsh nodded.

"What's your idea of Him? I mean everybody's got some different notions about who or what he is?"

Marsh pulled a blade of grass.

"It don't bother you talking about religion, does it? I mean some people—mighty store of 'em—don't like to talk about politics and religion. Me, never bothered me. I'm a Republican and I don't care who knows it.

Marsh split the blade of grass with his fingernail, pulled up another one and repeated the process. He stared at the grass a long time.

"Creator," he said after a moment.

"Oh, so you're not one of them evolutionists, then?"

Marsh shook his head.

"Me neither. That takes more stretch of imagination than the other." The old man leaned against the water fountain. "Creator, huh? That all? I mean you don't believe in no personal God?"

Marsh raised his eyes, looked at the old man a long time before responding.

"Do you?" he asked finally.

"Oh, you bet. Yeah, you bet I do. There's been the good times and the bad. But, yeah, there's a personal God. As personal as you make him.

That's what I always say."

Marsh continued to stare at the old man, looking through him. After a moment, the man unhooked his thumbs and shuffled on across the heavily-dewed grass toward the street bordering the back side of the park. His whistling grew fainter with each step.

Twenty-Two

"Come on, let's walk. It's not that far," Randi hollered to Mike as they left the side door of the school building.

"No. Let's drive. I'm parked over in the far lot."

"No." Randi pursed her lips and stopped dead-still, hands on her hips. "I want to walk." Her loose-fitting blouse fluttered in the slight breeze. She waited.

"Come on. You're being stubborn. It's six blocks down there." Mike waved his arm toward the Sonic.

"So?"

"Did your mother say it was okay?"

"Since when do I have to ask my mother if I can go get a coke after school?"

Mike turned around and came in her direction. Smiling triumphantly, Randi joined in step with him as they rounded the corner of the gym. Mike sauntered; Randi surged ahead, then slowed every few paces to wait for him.

"Why didn't you go in today—to the clinic?"

"My day off. For good behavior."

"Really."

"I'm serious. They said my body needed a rest from all that gook. I never knew anemia could be such a nuisance. And I thought the first day of tests was a pain—no pun intended."

Mike made no response.

They cut across the end of the baseball field where the team was practicing. Players, coaches, and on-lookers mingled freely around the edges of the diamond. Looking around for other friends on the sidelines, Randi stumbled on a bat lying in front of her.

"Watch out," Mike grabbed her arm.

"I just washed my feet, and I can't do a thing with 'em." She regained her balance without attracting attention from the group huddled nearby. She reached over, grabbed the bat as if to give it a fling in their direction, then turned to Mike.

"Here, get that ball there and throw me one." She backed up and slung the bat up to her shoulder. Mike didn't move.

"They're not using it," she coaxed. "Throw me a quick one." She backed further away from him, tossed another bat out of the way, and took a couple of practice swings.

"Come on. Put it down and let's go get

a coke."

"Just one. Please? Am I embarrassing you?"

"No." She backed a few steps further away. "I can't throw it that far—straight."

"Please."

"No."

She threw the bat down and stomped off ahead of him around the first base corner of the field. She got all the way into the street before she stopped and turned around; he took his time catching up to her.

"Now what's the temper all about?" he asked.

"Me? What's wrong with you?"

"Nothing's wrong with me. You're the one that's been acting like some . . . like some I don't know what."

"I am not. You could have just thrown me a ball."

"I didn't want to."

"Why not?"

"I just didn't."

Mike started off ahead of her this time down the sidewalk. Randi stood watching and then took out after him again. They walked along in silence. Their footsteps slapped the concrete in angry rhythm. Reaching the drive-in, she grabbed the door before he could open it and pushed inside. Without asking what she wanted, he ordered cokes. She took a seat in a booth near the window and waited.

Both sat drinking slowly, silent. Mike slid

back in the seat against the window, his back to the street scene. Randi studied his face, all signs of previous anger gone. His face glistened with beads of perspiration above where his hat band had been. His eyes avoided hers. He looked distracted, faraway, worried.

"You know, don't you?" she asked.

"Know what?"

"That's why you wouldn't throw me that ball and let me bat. And you didn't want to walk down here."

"I didn't feel like playing baseball, and I didn't want to leave the truck sitting in the school lot for some idiot freshman to come by and break off the mirror or antennae."

Randi never took her eyes off him. He still stared straight out across the room from his sideward position in the booth.

"Why can't you look at me?"

He turned his face toward her. "I'm looking."

"Who told you?"

"I don't know what you're talking about."

"Yes, you do. . . . And stop it. I'm not stupid. Somebody told you what's wrong with me, didn't they?"

Mike said nothing. He shook the ice in his cup from side to side, sipping slowly from first one side then the other.

"I bet it was Mother. When she called you that day and told you not to come by the clinic. Didn't she?"

"Look, Randi . . ." He set the cup down and

reached out to take her hand.

"Don't!" She stood up, knocking his drink over. Ice and coke ran in tiny streams to the edge of the table. Not waiting to clean it up, she stalked out the door, walked around the corner of the drive-in, and leaned up against the side of the building. Mike caught the swinging door and followed her around to the side.

"Why are you being like this?" he asked.

"Why did she tell you?"

"Your mother didn't tell me anything."

"Who told you?"

There was a long silence.

"Your dad."

"Daddy?"

Mike nodded. Randi leaned her head back against the brick wall and stared up at the sky, trying to blink away the tears.

"When?"

"A couple of weeks ago. He came by one afternoon when I was washing my truck."

"What did he say?"

"He . . . he just said you had . . . what was wrong with you. . . . And that you needed me. That's all."

"Well, I don't. You just don't feel sorry for me one bit."

"I'm not feeling sorry for you." He tried to take her arm and pull her to him, but she stood rigid against the wall, still looking up away from him.

"Yes, you are. And I don't need it. . . . How

long were you going to let me go on about the anemia before you told me you knew, huh?"

"Randi," he tried to coax her to him again, and then let her go as a car with several laughing and yelling kids pulled into the drive-in lane.

"You got a stubborn one, huh?" one of the kids yelled at them.

Mike looked in their direction and then back to Randi. "Come on, let's go." He walked off without further effort to touch her. She followed him back toward the street. Once on the sidewalk, he slowed down and turned to wait on her.

"Randi, I love you. I'm not staying with you because your dad asked me to."

"He asked you to do that?"

"No, I don't mean that. I just meant . . ."

"I don't want to ever go out with you again. Just leave me alone." Randi darted off ahead of him and ran panting along the side-street.

He shouted after her a couple of times, then gave it up. Slowly, he strode back toward the field house. Randi was leaning against his pickup when he got to the parking lot.

"Are you okay?"

"Yes, I'm okay," she snapped. Then, in a softer tone, "I forgot you have to take me home."

He unlocked the door on his side; she slid all the way across to the other side of the cab. They drove all the way to Ponderine without another word. Mike turned into her driveway.

"Please, don't tell anyone." Randi's voice was soft, childlike.

"Okay."

"Have you already?"

"No."

She reached for the door handle and jumped out before he'd fully stopped the truck.

Randi dialed, then listened to the phone ring several times. No answer. Her watch showed 4:30. She slammed the receiver down and stalked into the den to get her notebook. Her assignment sheets from the missed days listed two still unfinished papers. She worked two math problems, then folded the paper inside the book and laid it back on the TV. In her bedroom, she turned on the stereo and crawled up into the middle of the bed. Country-western lyrics filled the room for quarter of an hour. Back to the phone. This time her father answered.

"Why did you tell Mike?" she blurted into the receiver as soon as Marsh said hello.

The placid expression Marsh had worn into his office upon returning from the last patient visit faded.

"Tell him what?" He asked the question, knowing it was not going to work this time. Why had he said it? Her voice was cold, stiff, like an insurance clerk questioning a claim form.

"Mike told me you came by." She paused but didn't give him time to answer. Her voice no longer under control, she asked, "Why did you do it?"

"Baby, I . . . try to understand. I love you."

"Then why did you tell him?"

"I thought . . . you needed him to stand by you. . . . You were feeling so down when I was by the hospital that day."

"Why didn't you ask me what I wanted?"

Marsh said nothing.

"I don't understand. How could you do it?"

"Why are you so . . . angry? What did he say to you?"

"Nothing! He didn't say anything; he won't do anything. That's just it. You made him afraid of me—of what's going to happen to me."

"I didn't do any such thing!" Marsh's pitch matched his daughter's now.

"You did! He didn't even want to let me walk to the Sonic after school. He's afraid I'll get too tired or faint on him or something. He's afraid to be around me."

"Did he say that?"

"He didn't have to. It's written all over his face. He wouldn't throw me a ball. . . . He was afraid I'd get hit."

"I think maybe you're over-reacting. . . ."

"I am not. He was afraid of me. Can't you see what you did?"

"I'm sorry, Baby. All I wanted was for you to be . . . happy."

"Well, I'm not. And it's your fault. . . . Who else did you tell?"

"Now wait a minute. I didn't tell anybody else. And you can't blame me for this, this . . . situation." Marsh caught himself and slowed his speech. But his thoughts flashed ahead at lightning speed. He knew what was about to come through his lips, but was powerless to stop it. "Your mother's responsible for this."

"What do you mean?"

The thought was like a venomous spring pushing it's way into the atmosphere. "Your leukemia. Those reports everybody's talking about . . ."

"Yeah?"

"It was your mother who gave the newspaper the story and forced them out into the open."

"But that's good . . . isn't it? What's that got to do with me?" Randi was no longer crying; her voice, child-like again.

"She knew about the research when it was done, and she insisted on staying out here anyway. If she'd have spoken up—just told me—we'd have moved out of here ten years ago. Before . . . before this happened to you."

"She did?" Her voice was barely audible now.

Marsh held the receiver in silence, visualizing all too clearly in his mind Randi's anguished expression, wanting to recall his revelation.

"Randi? . . . I'm sorry."

"I have to go now." She lowered the receiver to its cradle and stood staring at her mother's hand-written notation protruding from behind the phone box, "Dr. Bateman—office 962-2234, Home 962-3698."

Twenty-Three

Gloria phoned Erin on Monday morning to say that she would be back in town early in the week and could they have lunch on Thursday. Checking her calendar, Erin realized that Thursday was her birthday. She didn't mention it. Yes, she'd told her, lunch would be fine.

As far as Erin knew, Marsh had made no plans for the occasion. Not that she'd expected him to. He'd come home for more of his clothes and said he was going to stay at Memorial for a few days. Their only communication since then had been to make arrangements for Randi's daily chemotherapy treatments. He'd suggested picking her up from school and taking her by the clinic. Erin brought her home after her observation period. The arrangement had worked fine.

Erin, in an affable mood, breezed into the office a little earlier than usual Thursday. Her parents had phoned to wish her happy birthday before she'd gotten out of bed. They always made a big deal of birthdays, even after she was grown and away from home.

Randi had been quiet at breakfast, giving her a voile blouse with little ceremony. Erin had tried it on immediately and expressed regret that she didn't have a skirt to match so she could wear it to work. Randi had shrugged; Erin promised to shop for a skirt on the weekend.

Although neither had verbally expressed it, both were aware of a warmer openness between them since Randi's learning about the leukemia. But in the last few days, their relationship had undergone a setback. Randi's conversation had been only perfunctory; she'd spent increasingly more time alone in her room. The new distance puzzled Erin. Maybe she'd discuss it with Gloria. Or, maybe they'd avoid the entire subject.

Freda tottered around the office at her usual pace. Erin had never mentioned her birthday to Freda or any employee; she hated the thought that they might feel obligated about a gift. Freda had mentioned birthdays once or twice when Erin had first taken over the department. But she'd managed to avoid giving her the date.

Her secretary buzzed to say Miss Delacourte was on the phone.

"You're going to hate me for this," Gloria said as soon as Erin came on the line.

"You can't go to lunch," Erin said flatly.

"Mr. Rowan came in first thing this morning and handed me another plane ticket."

"Well . . ." Erin tried to sift the disappointment from her voice, "the salad dressing probably would've been rotten anyway. This being near the end of the week and all."

"Yeah, . . . listen, I feel terrible about this after having you keep the date open all week."

"Oh, no problem."

"I'll call you when I get back next week. We'll set something up then. Maybe go shopping."

"Sounds good."

Erin hung up and glanced back to her desk. She slid the chair back abruptly and walked toward the window. A few leaves on her plants were turning; she stooped to the window ledge to yank them off, pulling them hard enough to upset part of the soil. She smirked, raked the dirt off into her hands, and dumped it into the trash.

Disappointment about a birthday was juvenile. No, it wasn't just that it was her birthday. She'd wanted to tell Gloria about Marsh's leaving. Something she hadn't mentioned to anyone else. Who else was there? Her own fault. She couldn't lay that on Marsh too. She sat back down to the papers on her desk. Her usual solution, wasn't it? It solved less and less.

"Aren't you going to eat lunch?" Freda stuck her head in her boss's doorway about 12:15.

Erin looked up. Her eyes burned with fatigue, yet she was completely absorbed in the material.

"I thought I'd work on through. I'm not quite finished with this."

"Oh," Freda said lamely, her red head bobbing to a slow stop.

"Why?"

"Just wondered. You're usually in the cafeteria by now, and I hadn't seen you leave." Freda, still holding the door ajar, looked back around into the hallway behind her. She nodded and then turned around again to face Erin. "Ralph wants to talk to you."

"Tell him to come on in."

"He's . . . down in the cafeteria. He wants you to come down there."

Erin shrugged, laid her pen down, and followed Freda down the hall. She was acting strangely, nervous, walking a few steps in front of her, saying nothing.

When they rounded the corner to the cafeteria, "Happy Birthday" shouts, claps, and whistles exploded. She stood looking around the room, astonished. Gloria, standing to the side of the back table, fluttered a wave toward her. So that's why the broken luncheon date.

Erin regained her composure, and Freda led her over to the table where everyone stood. She spied the large cake. "Happy Birthday, Boss" ballooned out from the mouth of a chocolate outlined computer.

"Well, I can't say you had a hard time figuring out where to catch me at lunch time." She paused and looked around the group. "This is . . ." she groped for a word, ". . . a surprise." She laughed. "How's that for being original?"

Ralph stepped over beside her and handed her one of the two packages he held. Here's hoping for everybody a raise."

Erin smiled again and took the gift. A gigantic envelope was taped to the top. She opened it first.

"How cute! Who's the artist?"

"Gilbert. But we all supplied the brain power."

The card was a caricature of Erin, well done. It showed her at her desk, an expression of deep concentration, with innumerable distractions clamoring for her attention. The caption read: "Three minutes for Ralph. Eight minutes for Freda. Six minutes for Mack," on and on with several names. Then, "I need some time away from the rat race. How about the cafeteria for lunch?"

"This is really cute, thanks." She laid it aside. "I guess my opening remark was appropriate." Then, pointing to the gift, "May I open this now?"

"Next Christmas," Ralph said.

She grinned and carefully tore into the first one. Then, glancing up toward Gloria as she worked with the scotch tape, "The boss just handed you a plane ticket, huh?"

Gloria spread her arms in a big shrug, bracelets on both arms jangling.

Erin turned toward Freda. "How'd you know to call her and get her to cancel our lunch date?"

"I didn't. She called me."

"What do you mean?" Ralph interrupted. "You don't think *we* planned any of this?" Erin ignored him and slipped the box out of the paper. It was a tiny gold chain; the ends hooked together in the front and hung loosely at the base of the neck in tie fashion.

"Oh, how pretty. Thank you so much." Erin took the necklace from the case and put it on. "It's beautiful."

Ralph held the second gift out to her. "This is a little heavier."

"I should say." Erin took it and began to unwrap it in the same cautious manner. Everyone was watching; she should say something. What? She smiled at herself; she just imagined she'd outgrown that innate shyness, insecurity. Only when she hid behind the desk. Her face felt flushed.

"You never did say how you found out it was my birthday," she directed the attention to Freda.

"Gloria. She called last Monday to say she'd asked you to lunch to make sure you'd be available and did we have anything planned."

"Did you tell her I'm always available?" Erin grinned. Gloria slipped around the table to her. "Well, then, who did this—you or them?"

"Both. As soon as they found when the big day was, Freda said everybody here would want to do something. Not that I was trying to get out of taking you to lunch. Freda said this was the only time everybody in the office could get together. You being the kind of boss you are."

"Ohhh," Erin nodded and slid the larger box from its wrapper.

"A salad bowl. It's beautiful." She held the cut-glass bowl up for the group to see. "It's really pretty. Thank you so much."

Applause. A few chants of "speech, speech."

"Well, needless to say, I'm still flabbergasted." She fidgeted with the wrapping paper. "It's been a good three years. . . ."

"How old?" someone interrupted.

Erin blushed, "Old enough to know better."

Everyone clapped again and the group began to disperse to their individual tables.

Erin gathered the gifts, card, and wrapping paper and walked over to where Freda and Ralph sat. "Thanks again. This was really sweet."

"And the raises?" Ralph asked.

Erin rolled her eyes at him and rejoined Gloria at the cake, which she was cutting into squares for everyone's dessert. Gloria monopolized the table, had taken charge completely. Her perfume floated in the air, amplified her lilting voice. Several men stood around trying to get her undivided attention.

"Well, shall we still go out to lunch? Shop for a while? Blow off the afternoon?" Gloria asked.

Erin shuffled the card and packages to the other arm and glanced at her watch. It was her birthday.

"Why not?" She followed Gloria out the cafeteria door.

"I'm not asking for the moon, am I?" Gloria asked. "Just a little more lavendar."

The clerk raised her already overly-arched eyebrows and cleared her throat. She nodded to the man on the phone. "We'll see."

Gloria and Erin leaned against the counter a moment and then took a seat near the desk where the salesman was busy with a telephone customer.

"Special order is my last hope," Gloria drawled.

"They can get it." Erin nodded. "They'll make up anything if the price is right."

Gloria grinned. Erin settled back in her seat. Deliciously idle. She had nothing to shop for. No price tags to check. No lines to wait in. They'd made three stops already for Gloria to find the nonexistant drapes she'd mentally created to go in her apartment with the new furniture.

After a moment, Gloria launched into a redescription of the color mixture she had in mind and exactly how each would help tie the room together. She continued to describe the ashtray she'd brought back from the last business trip. Knowing Erin liked decorating, she went into all the details of the bargains passed up and wondered if she should have chosen those instead. Erin answered in the appropriate pauses but kept losing the direction of the conversation. To fade in and out was easy; Gloria never minded filling up the silence.

Erin changed positions in the chair, slumped down a little further. Her arms felt limp, immoveable. Her mind drifted from part to part of her body—feet, legs, arms, neck, shoulders. Relax, relax, she coaxed. A day off. Was it really possible to disengage?

"Got a nail file I can borrow?" Gloria asked.

Erin rummaged through her purse and handed her the file.

"I'll tune back in in a minute," Gloria said. "I can't file and talk at the same time."

Erin grinned. A delusion of Gloria's. To think every silence begged for conversation. Erin settled back in the chair again, drinking in the thought of relaxation. Her birthday. The office party. All deadlines met for a change. She'd be starting with a clean slate tomorrow. A sense of euphoria flooded her senses; a tremor went up her spine.

Gloria finished and handed the file back to her.

"How much longer do you think the guy can be?" Gloria nodded to the salesman still talking on the phone.

"Not too long. He doesn't look like he knows that much."

"Got a point."

"That was really nice—about the cake and

the party," Erin said.

"You already said that."

"I mean it."

"I know. Forget it. You deserve a little attention. Employees take good bosses for granted. . . . You never did say what Marsh got you?"

"He didn't." Erin felt a weight fall to the pit of her stomach.

"Don't tell me he was poured out of that mold, too. Tell me, is that not the typical male reaction to birthdays—to forget?"

Erin turned her head toward the salesman. "Sounds like he's finishing up."

"Maybe. Say I haven't even got this all figured out yet. How much material I'm going to need?"

"They come out and measure and figure it for you."

"Yeah, I know. But I want some idea of how many yards so I can get a tentative figure in my head before I tell 'em what I really like. You have any idea how much it'll take?"

"Window measurements would help."

"Oh, sure." Gloria rummaged through her purse and handed the measurement figures to her. Erin sat figuring for a moment.

"Twelve and a half yards." She laid the pencil and paper down and slumped back into her chair.

Gloria studied Erin's calculations a moment, all neatly labeled as to widths and lengths and number of windows. Then she multiplied the yards times both the least and most expensively priced fabric she'd been shown. Erin watched her, but her mind floated, did not focus.

"Supermom, aren't you?" Gloria said when she finished.

"What?"

"Designer, musician, executive, wife, mother. Is there anything you can't do?"

"Just name the date, place, and time. Drop a nickle in and I perform."

"No kidding. I don't see how you do it all—I mean with Randi and everything."

"Randi's not the problem." The words came out abruptly. The "the" called for more explanation. Gloria waited. The weight again at the pit of her stomach. She sat up in the chair. Why couldn't she just throw it out, push the words out like so much garbage?

"Marsh's not at home, Gloria. He moved out."

Gloria's lips parted; she paused, studied her friend's eyes. "When? What happened?"

"Three weeks ago."

Silence.

"I've been thinking I'd call you. But. . . . He left the morning after you called about the newspaper story."

"Something about the story?"

"Yeah." Erin looked down again to her lap. Dump the whole thing. If she walks away . . .

"I told him I was the one who leaked the

story. That I'd known about the research for ten years. I saw the files way back when I was secretary for Morton." She studied her friend's face now as Gloria's eyes narrowed, her brow furrowed. Previous remarks from her about ecology matters, about the government's handling of such information echoed in her mind. She rushed ahead, "He kept telling me that the reports were inconclusive. That the government would come out with the final reports after the total investigation was completed. They never did."

Gloria nodded vigorously, an "I-told-you-so" look spread across her face.

"I just kept waiting, thinking, wondering. . . . You never think something like that will really happen—getting leukemia like that. You think somebody higher up knows what's going on and will do something about it."

There was a silence.

"So he just walked out?" Gloria asked. "He blames you for Randi?"

Erin nodded.

"He'll be back when he has time to think it through."

Erin considered the words as if for the first time. "I'm not sure that's what I want—right now."

Gloria shrugged.

"He's got his own problems. With himself." The words tumbled out now, as if a spring had been unclogged. "The roots were already loose even before this came up."

"Have you filed for divorce?"

"No."

Another silence.

"How's Randi taking it?"

"Like she takes everything else. In stride."

"Like her mother, huh? Don't look back?"

"I don't mean she doesn't miss him. But she's not . . . moping. Her grades are still up. But something's changed between them. I think the fact that he didn't tell her about the leukemia hurt her. . . . I don't know what it is; it's just not the same with them. But she and I were getting along so much better. After she came out of the hospital this time. But lately she's had little to say to me either. I figure she blames me for Marsh's leaving. Maybe she blames us both."

"She still sees him a lot?"

"Every day. He drives her to the clinic."

Silence.

"She gave me a blouse this morning for my birthday. Lavendar, in fact. That reminds me, I've got to look for a skirt if we have time after we finish here."

"I'm sorry ladies," the salesman moved toward them. A look of anguish spread across his face. "I had a long-distance customer. She calls me for everything she does. Trusts my judgment without even coming in." The salesman's sorrow at keeping them waiting thinly masked his pride. "Now what can I do for you?"

"Drapes. I need to special order some drapes," Gloria answered.

"Have you checked our ready-mades?"

"Lavendar."

"Oh." He flipped open the book of swatches.

Erin sat back in her chair. Gloria could pick out her own material. She closed her eyes, drifted away.

Twenty-Four

Erin walked into the same consultation office Marsh and she had entered so long ago; the chairs and sofa, jammed into the same arrangement. The announcement they'd heard that evening had played over and over in her mind until the doctor's voice had become a blur of sounds fading in and out of her consciousness. She could no longer recall how his words had first sounded. This time she had come alone.

Erin glanced up as her husband tapped on the door and walked in. He averted his eyes and took a seat in the chair near the desk. They sat for a few minutes in silence. Strangers.

Their eyes wandered around the room searching out a place to light. A calendar on the desk. No paintings. No decorative pieces. Not even an ashtray. Nothing to command attention.

"How have you been?" Erin asked finally.

Marsh glanced up at her, his eyes distant and guarded. "Okay."

"Are you still . . . staying at the hospital?" Erin almost stopped her question in midstream, afraid that he would interpret her inquiry as prying.

"No. A doctor at the hospital, Templar, owns some apartment buildings. He gave me a key to one."

"Oh." Then, "I guess that's a little more comfortable."

Marsh nodded and leaned forward, resting his forearms on his thighs. His body looked much too large for the chair.

They grew silent again. Marsh stared into empty space before him. Erin pulled a small spiral memo pad from her purse and studied it, but her mind paid no attention to the errands listed there. She guessed that Randi must have known about her dad's living arrangement but had chosen not to mention it to her.

"Good afternoon, Erin, Marsh." The doctor came in, walked between them, and took a seat behind the desk. "It seems you two are always having to wait for me."

Both Erin and Marsh attempted a smile.

The doctor continued, "I asked you to come to . . . let you know where we are with Randi. She's not in remission yet—as I'm sure you're well aware."

"She acts like she's feeling so much better," Erin remarked.

"Yes, she's really in good shape. Athletically.

That's a big help. Her determination is another thing in her favor."

"What are we going to do?" Erin asked.

"I wanted to explain some things to you this afternoon. The drug she's on doesn't seem to be doing the trick. We've got several routes we can go from here, but I want to tell you what we're considering, Dr. Skaggs and I. And let you discuss it . . . give you some time to think and plan."

Erin nodded again. Marsh continued to stare at the floor. The doctor went on, "As I said, we've got her on vincristine now, but it doesn't seem to be acting as fast as we'd hoped. We've had good results with it with other patients, but every patient's different. That's the whole ball game—what keeps us so confused. Anyway, we're going to give her another two or three weeks on it to see if it won't take a hold." He paused.

"Then what?" Erin asked.

"Then, I think we ought to take her to Anderson in Houston." He paused again, then continued. "There are very few places—Anderson's one—where they're really equipped to handle leukemia in anything but the traditional way—chemotherapy and drugs."

"What do you mean?" she asked.

"Well, we can try different drugs on her. Observe her for side-effects. Handle the effects of the less dangerous drugs. Do the bone marrow tests to see how she's progressing. . . . But when these common drugs are used to no avail, then . . . we need to send them somewhere else."

"What will they do there?"

"I don't know now—exactly. I work closely with a couple of doctors there at Anderson. In fact, I've already consulted them about Randi. They have the research going on right there. The very latest test results on new drugs and treatment. For instance, the laminar air-flow chamber—it was first used there."

Erin nodded; she had read every book in the Jackson library on leukemia and its treatment. In fact, a new one, which the librarian had just called her about, lay in her desk drawer.

The doctor continued about the air-flow chamber for Marsh's benefit. "That's a sterile chamber where they put a patient for protection from infection while his body defenses are so low. It's all an experimental program in the area . . ."

"What do you mean experimental?" Marsh spoke for the first time since the doctor had begun his explanations.

"Trying new drugs. New treatment. Like I just explained."

"But how experimental?"

"That it's not the conventional treatment of drug combinations and chemotherapy. It's experimental in the sense that the methods haven't been in use long enough to provide enough statistics to measure conclusively their effectiveness for different types of patients in various stages." He paused as if to wait for further questions from Marsh.

There were none; Marsh stared back down at the floor.

The doctor continued, "It'll help you on expenses some. Patients who participate in some of these programs have their drugs paid for by Uncle Sam."

"Well, at least that's one advantage," Erin mumbled. Marsh raised his head and glared at her.

"I'm not asking you to make the decision now. I still have hopes that this combination we've got her on will do the job in another week or two. I haven't gone into this much detail with you earlier because Randi responded so quickly before and achieved her first remission so soon." He paused. "But I did want you to think about what was ahead. To consider which route you'd like to go. . . . Are you . . . are there any questions about what I've said?"

"She acts like she feels okay. A little tired maybe, but . . ." Marsh groped for words to explain his lack of understanding how Randi could be so sick, yet so active.

"Yes. She's in good shape; she was when she came in here. That's been much to her advantage, as I said earlier. But in time . . . we need to get her into remission as soon as possible."

The doctor paused and scribbled on the chart lying on the desk. Finished with the notation, he looked up and waited to see if Erin and Marsh had any further questions. They didn't. He stood up, shook hands with Marsh, and headed toward the door.

"Think it over, and I'll be in touch with you."

"Thank you," Erin said. The door clicked shut behind him.

Brisk. Ten minutes, Erin noted, and all options became new.

Marsh leaned back in the straight-back chair, threw his head back, his chin out, then bent his head forward to touch his chest. For a few moments, he sat rubbing the back of his neck.

"Well?" he looked up abruptly. Erin studied his expression. His blue eyes looked darker, afraid. The muscles along his cheekline tremored. She noted his hair length, a little longer than usual.

"I thought this would work—the vincristine," Erin said aloud.

"He didn't say it wouldn't."

Erin stood up, walked over to the window, and gazed out at the sign in front of the entrance wing. They still could hear the same words and come up with different conclusions, meaning. She turned back to Marsh.

"If she goes to Anderson, at least some of the drugs and treatment would be paid for."

"Is that all you can think about—the money?"

"Of course, it isn't all I can think about!" Erin snapped. "I just said it was at least *one* favorable consideration. Somebody has to think about the money. I'd give every penny we have or could borrow. . . . Have you checked our savings account lately? We don't have much left to give. What then, Marsh? You've got to think about what then."

He got up from his chair and began to lumber around the room, both hands in his pockets, keys jangling. "I just don't like the idea of an experimental anything."

"Well, it's not like they haven't used the drugs and treatment on anybody. Hundreds go through the program."

"Not enough. Not enough to have proven results," Marsh corrected her.

"But it's a chance; she's not responding here."

"That depends."

"I think we should trust Dr. Bateman's judgment—not to do anything that would be dangerous or . . ."

"Not dangerous?" he looked at her incredulously. "Not dangerous? Did you say not dangerous?"

"I meant they'd keep close watch on her, monitor her reactions," Erin was almost shouting.

Marsh turned around and paced in the other direction. Erin leaned against the window casement, arms folded across her waist to quiet the gnawing pain in her abdomen.

Marsh stopped pacing as he approached Erin's end of the room again. "I'll go with her if she goes."

"So will I," Erin said.

"It won't be necessary for both of us to go. It might be several weeks."

"I said I wanted to go, too," Erin repeated.

Marsh's monotonous pace continued. Up, back. Up, back. The office was small; he had less than six steps in either direction.

"We could be wasting time with her here . . . using drug after drug, waiting for it to take effect. At least there, we'd know they had the best, latest things."

"Let them use her for guinea pig in other words? Treat these fifty patients with one drug, the next fifty with a different drug and congratulate the winners. Is that what you want to do?"

"No, I . . ."

"Go ahead. Experiment with her. That's your thing, isn't it? Our living here is your one big experiment, Erin. . . . Have the results been interesting?"

Erin picked up her purse from the sofa and walked out.

Twenty-Five

Ten days later, Dr. Bateman called to say that Randi was in her second remission. The medicine had finally taken hold of the disease; the bone marrow showed no abnormal cells.

"Let's celebrate," Marsh shouted into the phone when Randi called him at the office. "Let's . . . let's go out to dinner and a movie."

"Okay. Just a minute, let me ask Mother?" She paused, "You mean all of us?"

"Yeah, sure."

Randi covered up the receiver and shouted to her mother, who'd just come home from work. "Daddy says let's celebrate. He wants us to go to dinner and a movie."

Erin finished taking off her earrings and laid them in her jewelry box. "Okay," she shouted from the bedroom. When Dr. Bateman had called to tell her the news, she'd been elated. The fatigue drifted away as her mental spirits soared. She'd rounded up her work to a stopping point and left to get home an hour earlier than usual. She thought of calling Marsh, but Randi would enjoy doing that.

"I'll pick you two up at 7:00, how's that?"

"Great. Where we going?"

"You pick the place. Sky's the limit."

"Okay. But you don't know what you're saying."

Erin was ready early. She sat on the couch, painting her fingernails by lamplight. She wore the dark coral dress Marsh had given her Christmas two years ago. She'd changed clothes several times before deciding. Wearing the dress, his favorite, meant different things as her mood changed. What was she trying to say to him? That she still cared? That she could wear it with no feeling at all? She wasn't sure herself. When he walked in, she'd know.

Randi came into the den and sat down on the other end of the couch. Their perfumes filled the air, clashed. She watched Erin apply the second coat of polish.

"When's Daddy coming back—to stay?"

Erin looked up. "I don't know." Randi looked away. "I guess that's up to your dad."

Randi got up and turned on the TV.

Erin and she had still not discussed the subject of Marsh's absence more than to mutually acknowledge the fact that he was gone, that he was staying somewhere else "for a while." In other mother-daughter relationships, the silence might have become too great to be sustained. As it was, the lack of explanation each to the other was a life-long pattern.

Erin longed for the openness they'd shared briefly—ever since that day in the hospital when she'd told her about the leukemia. Randi gave her no indication what had altered the relationship again for the worse.

Even though not at home in the evenings, Marsh saw Randi daily. In addition to driving her to the clinic for treatments, he'd picked her girlfriends and her up from school a couple of days to take them to lunch. Despite these contacts, neither had discussed the past weeks' living arrangements. Marsh had attributed Randi's sullenness to her frustrations over making the daily trips to the clinic and missing her usual after-school activities.

When Marsh arrived at the house a little before 7:00, he felt strange. What to do? Should he go in the back or front? Knock or just walk in? It was his house. Having not yet used the word "separation" to explain the situation, he was at a loss to explain his hesitancy about entering. People certainly would walk out on his counseling sessions if they knew he couldn't hold his own marriage together, couldn't follow his own advice. Steve and Sandy had been in again earlier in the week and seemed well on their way to working things out. She'd managed to get her duty changed to another floor and had standard hours in the daytime, no more shifts. If only Erin and he could find it that simple. He decided on the back door.

Knocking loudly, he walked in without

waiting for an answer. Both Erin and he spoke simultaneously.

"Hi, Daddy," Randi shot up from her chair and turned off the TV.

"You look gorgeous," Marsh said to Randi.

"Thanks. But wait until you hear where I've decided you're taking us."

"Okay. Scratch one compliment. Where?"

"The Wharf."

"Sounds great."

"The lobster's outa sight. Mike took me there once before, remember?" A flicker of anxiety spread across Marsh's face.

All three left the house together to celebrate their new dream—that this remission would never end. It was more than a dream; it was their conscious plan. But the silence was somewhat strained, especially in the beginning. Scars from long-past conversations rose above the smooth surface of congeniality; they were far from healed.

During the meal, Randi and her upcoming plans remained the focal point.

"I called Meganne to tell her I'd be staying after school to plan the Spanish club fiesta. That'll be our last party before school's out."

"What kind of planning?" Erin asked.

"You know, decorations, theme, menu, stuff like that. We get to decide it all—as long as our money holds out."

Randi flitted to other topics of conversation—primarily, where she might find a summer job if Hayden's wouldn't let her come back to work there. Both Erin and Marsh let the topic pass with the same resignation as to her previous working venture.

"Do you think you're about ready for a car?" Marsh asked during the cheesecake dessert.

"Are you kidding?"

Randi looked from Marsh to Erin.

"Does your dad already have something picked out?" Erin asked, looking at Marsh.

"No, I've done a little looking, but we'll need to take our time, get something we really want."

Erin noted the "we," felt better, smiled.

Randi and Marsh carried on a dialogue about what makes and models would be first on their shopping list. Randi wanted something sporty all right, but with good gas mileage—for the future when she was away at college putting in her own gas. Marsh suggested the want-ads as a place to start the search. Randi said she didn't want to "rush things"—so that she could get what she really wanted. Erin smiled. At least that much of her rubbed off on her. She'd always considered her own practicality a fault. To Marsh, it was.

There was a pause in the conversation as they finished the cheesecake.

Randi spoke, her voice barely audible, "This is so good."

"Uh huh," Erin took the last bite and looked up.

"Tonight, I mean." Randi's eyes glistened.

There was silence.

"Well, what movie do you have picked out?"

Marsh asked.

"A good one. I've seen the previews. And Mike was talking about it in school today."

She reviewed the story briefly to them. They rose to go. Randi waited for Erin to get in the front seat first between her and her dad. On the way to the cinema, they were quiet again. The atmosphere was cordial, yet Erin felt as if every movement or word between them was being weighed.

Marsh's shoulder pressed against hers as they turned a corner. Neither moved apart. They rode along in silence except for the stereo.

When they filed into the theater seats, Marsh paused in the aisle and let Randi and her pass into the row in front of him. They sat down with Randi in the middle. The movie was a tender love story, boy meets girl variety.

"Would you two like to stop for something else to eat?" Marsh asked when they were back in the car.

"I couldn't eat another bite," Randi answered.

"How about you, Erin?"

"No, me either."

Comments about the movie and the promised car sprinkled their trip home. Randi rehearsed again the plans for the week and the rest of the school year. Gradually, the comments grew less frequent, each settled into his own thoughts. The flashing neon lights of Jackson faded into the starlit highway to Ponderine. The motor's hum mesmerized as they all three watched the road ahead.

The evening was over. Marsh deposited them at the front door. The motor still idled.

"Aren't you coming in—for a while?" Randi asked.

Erin had headed toward the door. Marsh hesitated for a moment, then shook his head. Randi slid over toward her mother's side of the car and stepped out. He left the car lights on them while they got inside. Then he was gone.

In the kitchen, Randi shuffled from side to side opening and closing cabinet doors. Thumbing through the mail again, Erin watched her out of the corner of her eye. What was she thinking, feeling? Finally Randi wandered off toward her bedroom empty-handed; Erin watched her go. Neither had spoken since leaving the car. Why had she shut her out again? Obviously, she blamed her for Marsh's absence. Certainly Marsh's refusal to come in disappointed her. Maybe she should've been the one to ask him in. She'd thought about it earlier, had almost decided she would, then rejected the idea. He'd been the one to leave; it was his decision to come back—even for an evening. She'd been through the worst alone. The earlier tingle of anticipation vanished. She felt emotionally numb.

She put down the mail and followed Randi down the hall to her own bedroom. The stereo from Randi's room filled the house with strains of some album Erin didn't recognize. She dotted cleansing cream on her face and began to remove make-up.

Tonight had been good, like Randi had said. Marsh had even been jovial. His anger toward her seemed diminished, or maybe just buried. Erin turned over in her mind various points of the evening's converstation, trying to decide which.

Her eye caught the mirror image of his broken electric razor sitting on the bureau behind her. She'd noted earlier in the evening that he'd had a fresh shave. Something he rarely did—shave again in the evening. Was it for her? She stared into the mirror, but saw Marsh's face reflected there. She could almost feel his arms around her, softly kissing the back of her neck, then turning her around to kiss her full on the mouth. She ached. She wanted to stretch. Scream at the top of her lungs, punch a hole in the wall. She shuddered.

"Mother?"

"Yes?"

"Can I come in?"

"Uh huh."

Erin tissued the last smear of cleansing cream from her face. Randi sat down on the edge of the bed, then got up, pulled back the spread, and took her seat for the second time. Erin brushed her teeth while Randi sat watching her. Finishing, she looked up to see Randi's fixed gazed on her.

How often she'd dreamed her daughter would

come into her room, sprawl out on the bed, and talk until early morning. Erin's heart pounded faster as she watched Randi out of the corner of her eye. Gathering her clothes from the other side of the bed, she hung her dress and put away her shoes.

"I'm glad I'm in remission now. . . . I can quit thinking about it, you know? Having to go by the clinic every day."

"Me, too, Honey."

"It's gonna last this time."

Erin smiled and nodded again.

Randi lowered her eyes and pulled on the long, dingy white thread stitched around the well-worn sole of her houseshoe. Her toe stuck through a two-inch gap.

"If there was just . . . if they knew what caused it—the leukemia, in the first place—looks like they could find a cure."

The thud against Erin's chest quickened. She laid her slip aside on the dresser and sat down on the edge of the bed. Randi never looked up; she examined the unraveling shoe.

"I mentioned before that they thought it was some sort of virus . . ." she paused, still watching Randi's downturned face, "or in some cases, radiation in the air."

"Cases like mine?" Randi's voice was soft, almost whisper level.

Erin reached over and pulled Randi to her shoulder. Tears came freely now for both. Erin sat hugging, rocking her daughter from side to side.

"Daddy said you knew. He said that you're the one that gave the news story to the papers. He said you knew all the time."

"Randi, look at me." She let her mother's hand gently lead her chin upward until their eyes met. "I want to explain."

Randi looked directly into her mother's face. Waiting.

"I saw the leukemia-radiation study when I first started to work for Bending. And I was scared. But my boss told me the reports were unimportant, inconclusive—that other studies between radiation and leukemia showed no danger at all." Erin paused. Then, "He told me that the government would publish something about it—if the reports were really true. I kept waiting . . . But nobody ever said or did anything about it."

Erin dropped her hand from Randi's chin.

"But you still wanted to stay here, didn't you?"

"Yes. Yes, I did. Very badly. I liked my job and had a good chance to be promoted. And I was almost through with school. . . . But I'd have left in a minute—if it could have changed anything. It was too late—even then. The testing had already moved underground. The damage had already been done."

"But why didn't you tell us? Daddy?"

Erin looked away from Randi's piercing stare for the first time. "Telling him . . . telling him would have only made him angrier at me for insisting we live here." She turned back to her daughter.

Randi leaned into her mother's arms. "But why me?" she sobbed, her face buried in her mother's shoulder. "Just why me?"

Erin rocked her daughter in her arms.

Twenty-Six

"*¿Cómo estás?*" Randi greeted Meganne.

"*Estoy bien*".

"Well, it's nice to see you two have mastered the first day's work," Vonna commented from her perch atop the lunchroom table.

"Look," Meganne said, "'How are you' and 'I'm fine' is just about as proficient as I'll ever get in a foreign language."

"You aren't going to take it next year?"

"Are you kidding?"

"Well, I'm taking it again for sure," Randi said. "I figure three years of it will get me into anywhere I decide to go to college."

Randi printed *Fiesta Grande* across the top of her poster, then stopped. "This has the menu on it. Are we going to put the menu on it—on a poster?"

"Sure. That's what everybody's coming for."

Randi shrugged and printed the menu with

alternating colored markers.

"I should get you two to help me make posters for the cheerleading tryouts next week," Vonna said, never looking up from her work.

Both Meganne and Randi glared at her. "Are you trying out?"

"No. Just kidding. I just thought I'd see what you'd say. I wouldn't get out there for anything. But I sure do think *one* of us oughta try out."

Vincent and Mike came through the cafeteria door.

"What're you doing in here?" Mike asked.

"The *Fiesta Grande* is now in its final planning stage. Better speak now or forever hold your peace," Meganne called to them.

"I'm not coming," Vince said.

"Well, in that case, you can work on Vonna's cheerleading posters."

"You tryin' out?"

"No. I'm not trying out. I was just kidding."

"Well, one of you ought to. I'm tired of the same old ones getting everything."

"That's what I say. Randi. We oughta get Randi out there. Get a few brains on the squad for a change. And she's got a good figure. That's ninety percent of it right there. Isn't it, Vince."

"Sure. But who needs brains to yell?" He shrugged and slumped back on the end of the table.

"I'm not kidding. I think you oughta try out.

You were a cheerleader in junior high, weren't you?"

"So were a lot of other people," Randi said.

"I think you should, too," Mike added. Randi's cheeks flushed; she finished the menu list. Although they saw each other frequently and still had mutual friends, he had not asked her out since their discussion at the Sonic. Neither had he dated anyone else. She had given him no reason not to take her at her word.

"Everybody who thinks Randi ought to try out, say 'aye,'" Meganne said.

"Aye," the others responded.

"Forget it."

Erin came home to find Randi sitting in the grass in the middle of the backyard. She noted the heavy breathing and the flush of her cheeks.

"What are you doing?"

"Turning a few flips to see if I remember how."

"Do you?"

"Pretty much. But I need somebody else to practice with. To throw me up and all."

"Sorry, but I don't think I could quite fit the bill."

"Well, I didn't mean you."

"Why all the interest in flips?"

Randi tugged at the tongue in her tennis shoe and decided to relace it. Her hair hung forward and partially hid her face. She took her time before answering.

"I don't know. . . . Meganne and Vonna were saying I should try out for cheerleaders next year. Tryouts are next week."

"Hmmm."

Randi looked up at Erin, who was leaning against the door casement.

"What are you thinking?" Randi asked.

"Nothing yet. I hadn't thought about it."

There was a pause.

"But I was also thinking it wouldn't be fair." Randi glanced back down to finish the relacing job.

"Not fair?"

"Having people vote for me because they felt sorry for me."

"Why do you think that?"

"A lot of 'em know I've had to leave school every day to go to the clinic. . . . I'm just afraid . . . I keep thinking Mike might tell somebody, or somebody at the clinic will say something, you know?"

"Well, if it happens, it happens. But there's no way anybody could say you were *trying* to get sympathy."

Randi locked her arms around her knees. "Do you think I'd have a chance—really?"

"I don't see why not. You're still as good as you were in junior high. And everybody knows your name from basketball."

"Yeah."

Erin's vision blurred as she watched her

daughter turn a perfect cartwheel and then land in a split. The muscles in her thighs tightened. No stress on her face, discomfort. What was the difference between remission and cured? She blinked a few times and was in control again.

Twenty-Seven

Ralph stood waiting by Erin's doorway for her to sign a letter to go out with the morning mail. Erin shook her head; he always wore a half grin, as if remembering an old joke. Following him in, Freda carried two folders of typed reports ready for her to read final copy and approve. Erin was three pages into the first one when Marsh phoned.

"I'd like to meet you for lunch."

"Okay. . . . Where?"

"Flanagin's. About 2:00."

"All right."

"See you then." He hung up.

Having trouble concentrating on the reports before her, Erin read and reread several pages. What did he want? Had he thought things over? She wasn't sure she had. Did she want him back? She answered that question differently almost daily. The decision she'd made so long ago—to refuse to see divorce as an alternative—now seemed like one made in another era, in another relationship altogether. He'd given nothing since Randi's illness—not understanding, not support, not even his presence.

Maybe that wasn't what he wanted at all. Their dinner and movie celebration certainly gave no indication that coming home was on his mind. After the last few days' re-evaluation of the evening, she'd decided that the warmth was all for Randi's sake.

Maybe the talk about the news story bothered him. Well, if she could take it, he could. She approved Ralph's work and left the office.

She drove unconscious of the wheel in her hand. She felt like a sky diver. Falling. Falling. Then the fall broke into a floating sensation. All emotion floated from her body. For a long time, she merely drove. No thoughts. No hopes. No fears. Nothing.

The restaurant was almost cleared out by the time she arrived. She paused to let her eyes adjust to the dimness. The buffet table looked sparse, bland, like leftover cold cuts from an office party. Marsh waited at a table in the far corner, partially hidden by a large fern. As she approached, he stood and pulled out a chair for her.

"Well, you're right on time. . . . As always." He swallowed the last phrase. Erin smiled tightly and sat down.

"I hope this wasn't too inconvenient? That

you weren't too busy."

"No."

"It's a little later than you usually eat, I mean."

"It's fine."

Silence.

Erin reached across the table, opened a menu and studied it. "I'll have a salad."

"Are you sure that's all?"

She nodded.

The waitress took the order and returned promptly with the food. They ate with minimal conversation. Marsh asked if Randi enjoyed their evening together; Erin assured him that she had. Erin asked about a couple of his longterm patients; Marsh answered that they were doing as well as expected, that one had gone home over a month ago. Topics came and went; they lapsed into uneasy silence after each. Their faces bore no more than "we need new tires for the car" expressions.

Finished with their meal, they lapsed into silence again. Erin sat at a loss. Was this all he wanted? A friendly chat? Why today? Could it ever be the same with the blame she knew he still harbored?

She glanced toward the young couple sitting at the next table. They leaned toward each other as they spoke; the woman's lips were screwed into a provocative pout. His eyes caressed her. The lighted globe in the center of their table threw back Erin's own reflection. She remembered a similar luncheon, a similar era in Marsh's and her life. She'd dropped by his office unexpectedly, crawled into his lap, asked to be taken to lunch. Before the waitress had even brought their food, she'd given him the news that she was pregnant. Marsh had moved around to her side of the table, made a real lover's scene. She hadn't cared, had been as thrilled as he.

The couple seated at the next table rose to go. Erin's eyes followed them out; it was as if she had failed to say goodbye to a part of herself. She lowered her eyes to the beige linen tablecloth, traced its pattern to the corner of the table.

"Erin, I want a divorce."

She raised her eyes to his. "That's quite a statement to drop between the soup and salad." The corners of her mouth turned up briefly.

"I can't forget, Erin. . . . I can't.

She held his stare for a moment. Then he looked away, dropped his eyes to the empty dishes in front of him. She still stared at his downcast face. Was that what the words really sounded like? That simple? I want a divorce, Erin. No weight, no tears, no bitterness. Simply a fact. No one around them would suspect anything strange about their luncheon date, their voices, their faces. Eighteen years.

Scenes raced through her mind. The wedding reception line. Shaking hands with high school friends, aunts, uncles. Pizza at midnight, the first she'd ever made from scratch. She'd finished cleaning up the kitchen at 2:00. The campout when the tent had fallen in on them in the middle of the night. Their fifth wedding anniversary when they'd spent the day shopping for a piano. Spare no expense, he'd said. Get the best. The argument over where to put the tree in the backyard. The celebration when the bank called to say they'd made a hundred dollar error and would be crediting their account. Their monthly arguments about checks not recorded in the checkbook register. Randi's first birthday party. Her trying to hold the party hat on Randi's head while Marsh took the pictures. The accusations about the blurred ones when they got the prints developed. The bicycle which Marsh had spent almost all night putting together. It had been ten dollars cheaper in the carton than assembled. The lovemaking. The smell of his cologne when he climbed into bed. The warmth of his embrace when she lay with her back to him and he slipped his arms around her waist, pulled her close to him. An eighteen-year panorama. Over.

Marsh looked up again. Was there a point in challenging, contradicting, convicting, crushing? She decided not. His eyes were vacuous. Grief consumed him; nothing remained.

"All right, Marsh."

He paused a moment longer, then slowly picked up the check and walked away.

"Take these into Erin as you go." Freda

handed a graph and two summary pages to Ralph. "These are the figures on the flex-time survey."

Ralph took the pages in his free hand and backed through her doorway.

"Santa Claus, I presume?" Erin asked.

"With all kinds of goodies here. First and foremost," Ralph's pompous voice rose, "check out those figures." Erin looked over the graph.

"Every single company that had us do the survey. And those are statewide."

"Well," Erin took one last look. "There's just one major error...."

"What's that? Where?" Ralph leaned over her desk to examine the graph again. The smell of peanut butter-cheese crackers filled the air between them.

"No. No. I'm kidding."

Ralph slumped back into the sofa behind him.

"They look great. Give them to Freda, have her make copies, and send them out." She handed the report and graphs back to Ralph, who took them but made no attempt to leave.

"I saw your 'for sale' sign up in the yard when I passed this morning."

She nodded and slid her fingers up and down the pencil, rotating it end to end on the desk. He was the first who'd noticed—or at least the first to mention it. She didn't know which.

Marsh had transferred the last of his things from the house into a small apartment near

Memorial. But a week after he'd moved in there, he'd submitted his resignation as chaplain. The information about his resignation had come to Erin by way of Randi. He'd called once—to tell her to do whatever she wanted about the house.

"I hope it doesn't take too long to sell," Erin finally added. "I'm going apartment hunting this weekend."

"Better not let that house go until you get an apartment. I hear they're hard to come by. Decent ones."

"So I've heard."

"But you won't have trouble selling your house. It's a seller's market right now. Surprisingly. After the papers got through with that radiation story, I expected to see a mass exodus."

The telephone buzzed.

"Excuse me a minute." Erin picked up the receiver.

"Mother?"

"Randi, where are you?"

"School."

"But what's . . . aren't you in class?"

"I was. But Hoakum got sick and they couldn't get a substitute so late in the morning. Next to the last day of school and everything. So they told our class we could go on to lunch early."

"Well, that's a break."

"Not really. Who wants to eat lunch by yourself. Nobody I run with is in there."

"Oh."

"So I'm hanging around until regular lunch period. I was down here by the phones. Thought I'd call and see what you were doing. You have time to talk?"

"Sure." Tears formed in Erin's eyes; she turned slightly so Ralph couldn't see her face. "They couldn't find a substitute, huh? . . ."

BESTSELLERS FOR TODAY'S WOMAN

THE BUTTERFLY SECRET (394, $2.50)
By Toni Tucci
Every woman's fantasy comes to life in Toni Tucci's guide to new life for the mature woman. Learn the secret of love, happiness and excitement, and how to fulfill your own needs while satisfying your mate's.

BELLA (498, $2.50)
by William Black
A heart-warming family saga of an immigrant woman who comes to America at the turn of the century and fights her way to the top of the fashion world.

SARAH'S AWAKENING (536, $2.50)
By Susan V. Billings
From the insecurities of adolescence through the excitement of womanhood, Sarah goes on a wild, wonderful, yet sometimes frightening sexual journey searching for the love and approval of one very special man.

FACADES (500, $2.50)
By Stanley Levine & Bud Knight
The glamourous, glittering world of Seventh Avenue unfolds around famous fashion designer Stephen Rich, who dresses and undresses the most beautiful people in the world.

LONG NIGHT (515, $2.25)
By P. B. Gallagher
An innocent relationship turns into a horrifying nightmare when a beautiful young woman falls victim to a confused man seeking revenge for his father's death.

Available wherever paperbacks are sold, or order direct from the Publisher. Send cover price plus 40¢ per copy for mailing and handling to Zebra Books, 21 East 40th Street, New York, N.Y. 10016. DO NOT SEND CASH!

FICTION FOR TODAY'S WOMAN

THE BUTTERFLY SECRET (394, $2.50)
by Toni Tucci
Every woman's fantasy comes to life in Toni Tucci's guide to new life for the mature woman. Learn the secret of love, happiness and excitement, and how to fulfill your own needs while satisfying your mate's.

FACADES (500, $2.50)
by Stanley Levine & Bud Knight
The glamourous, glittering world of Seventh Avenue unfolds around famous fashion designer Stephen Rich, who dresses and undresses the most beautiful people in the world.

LONG NIGHT (515, $2.25)
by P. B. Gallagher
An innocent relationship turns into a horrifying nightmare when a beautiful young-woman falls victim to a confused man seeking revenge for his father's death.

BELLA'S BLESSINGS (562, $2.50)
by William Black
From the Roaring Twenties to the dark Depression years. Three generations of an unforgettable family—their passions, triumphs and tragedies.

MIRABEAU PLANTATION (596, $2.50)
by Marcia Meredith
Crystal must rescue her plantation from its handsome holder even at the expense of losing his love. A sweeping plantation novel about love, war, and a passion that would never die.

Available wherever paperbacks are sold, or order direct from the Publisher. Send cover price plus 50¢ per copy for mailing and handling to Zebra Books, 21 East 40th Street, New York, N.Y. 10016. DO NOT SEND CASH!

BESTSELLERS FOR TODAY'S WOMAN

ALL THE WAY (571, $2.25)
by Felice Buckvar
After over twenty years of devotion to another man, Phyllis finds herself helplessly in love, once again, with that same tall, handsome high school sweetheart who had loved her . . . ALL THE WAY.

HAPPILY EVERY AFTER (595, $2.25)
by Felice Buckvar
Disillusioned with her husband, her children and her life, Dorothy Fine begins to search for her own identity . . . and discovers that it's not too late to love and live again.

SO LITTLE TIME (585, $2.50)
by Sharon M. Combes
Darcey must put her love and courage to the test when she learns that her fiancé has only months to live. Destined to become this year's *Love Story*.

RHINELANDER PAVILLION (572, $2.50)
by Barbara Harrison
A powerful novel that captures the real-life drama of a big city hospital and its dedicated staff who become caught up in their own passions and desires.

THE BUTTERFLY SECRET (394, $2.50)
by Toni Tucci
Every woman's fantasy comes to life in Toni Tucci's guide to new life for the mature woman. Learn the secret of love, happiness and excitement, and how to fulfill your own needs while satisfying your mate's.

Available wherever paperbacks are sold, or order direct from the Publisher. Send cover price plus 50¢ per copy for mailing and handling to Zebra Books, 21 East 40th Street, New York, N.Y. 10016. DO NOT SEND CASH!

BESTSELLERS FOR TODAY'S WOMAN

THE VOW (653, $2.50)
by Maria B. Fogelin
On the verge of marriage, a young woman is tragically blinded and mangled in a car accident. Struggling against tremendous odds to survive, she finds the courage to live, but will she ever find the courage to love?

FRIENDS (645, $2.25)
by Elieba Levine
Edith and Sarah had been friends for thirty years, sharing all their secrets and fantasies. No one ever thought that a bond as close as theirs could be broken... but now underneath the friendship and love is jealousy, anger, and hate.

CHARGE NURSE (663, $2.50)
by Patricia Rae
Kay Strom was Charge Nurse in the Intensive Care Unit and was trained to deal with the incredible pressures of life-and-death situations. But the one thing she couldn't handle was her passionate emotions... when she found herself falling in love with two different men!

RHINELANDER PAVILLION (572, $2.50)
by Barbara Harrison
Rhinelander Pavillion was a big city hospital pulsating with the constant struggles of life and death. Its dedicated staff of overworked professionals were caught up in the unsteady charts of their own passions and desires—yet they all needed medicine to survive.

Available wherever paperbacks are sold, or order direct from the Publisher. Send cover price plus 50¢ per copy for mailing and handling to Zebra Books, 21 East 40th Street, New York, N.Y. 10016. DO NOT SEND CASH!